DOUBLED PLEASURE

Eli Holten stared at the two divine young women and opened his mouth to speak, but no words would form. Oblivious to his amazement, Beth said:

"Eli, dear, this is my sister, Bonny. But of course you've met her before."

"I have?" Eli managed.

"Sure you have," Bonny cooed. "Beth and I have been, uh . . . trading off over the past few days."

"Twins," Eli forced out, his head swimming.

"Absolutely identical," Beth said.

Holten's knees felt weak. "Then you've been . . . and I've been . . . but what about tonight?"

"You get . . ." Bonny began.

"Both of us . . ." Beth added.

"Together!" they completed in chorus.

WHITE SQUAW
Zebra's Adult Western Series
by E.J. Hunter

Available wherever paperbacks are sold, or order direct from the Publisher. Send cover price plus 50¢ per copy for mailing and handling to Zebra Books, Dept. 1898, 475 Park Avenue South, New York, N.Y. 10016. Residents of New York, New Jersey and Pennsylvania must include sales tax. DO NOT SEND CASH.

#22

THE SCOUT

RAILHEAD ROUND-UP

BY BUCK GENTRY

ZEBRA BOOKS
KENSINGTON PUBLISHING CORP.

Special thanks to Mark K. Roberts for his assistance in developing this book.

ZEBRA BOOKS

are published by

Kensington Publishing Corp.
475 Park Avenue South
New York, NY 10016

First printing: September 1986

Printed in the United States of America

This volume is dedicated to a gifted author and good friend, Dixie Lee McKeon, who has been overlooked too long. Bless her!

BG

"*The regular frontier scouts rarely provided their services to the railroads. Their close bonds with the Indians they frequently led troops in search of caused them to feel like the redman . . . that the iron rails spelled an end to their way of life.*"

—Gen. Granville Dodge
· *The Union Pacific*

Chapter 1

Spotted Horse of the *Mahohewas*, Red Shields — the Bull Soldier society — crouched below the brow of the ridge that separated him from his enemy. A member of the *Issio me tan iu* tribal band, he had journeyed far to bring this fight to the *nia'tha* below. It would be good to hurt them. For they deserved it.

Once the *Tsistsistas* rode free over all this land, Spotted Horse thought as he looked down the long slope to the small, stick-figures who swarmed around the end of the iron road. We came here before even our cousins, the Dakota. Some say that our Red Paint People fought against the Dakota. If it is so, it happened many seasons beyond the memory of any man living. Spotted Horse's reflections turned sour.

After our cousins, came the *nia'tha*, the cursed white men. From horizon to horizon, they filled this land like so many locusts. They have brought one iron road, that cuts the prairie in two through the heart of what was once our home, to the south of this place. Then came the one to the north. It divided the buffalo herds. Sent us to the west. Now these iron bands spread outward to cut the prairie again. It cannot be so, Spotted Horse's anger dictated.

It would not be. Although late in the seasons, in fact well into *Seine*, the Moon when the water begins to freeze on the edge of streams, he would take the fight to the *nia'tha*. Quickly he withdrew and swung atop his favorite war pony. Spotted Horse looked along the silent, grim-faced line of Cheyenne warriors. Many had offered to follow the sacred pipe of war he carried. That, too, was good. He raised his arm in signal and the attack began.

Sweat dripped from his forehead and stained the armpits of his shirt. Sean O'Casey paused after the final swing that set the spike into a fresh tie. He breathed deeply and let the air out in a whistling sigh. Mary and all the Saints, he thought. Here it was mid-October and still the sun beat down like the furnace of hell. Sean had worked for the railroads since the age of fifteen. Never before, though, had he encountered such wretched weather as here on the prairie.

Hot as Hades for five or six months, then cold as a harlot's heart for the rest of the year. Only a bloody fool would want to live here. Sean would be glad when the job ended. Since he had obtained his growth—not particularly impressive at five-foot-seven and a hundred-thirty pounds—Sean had been a gandy dancer. He laid track for the ever-expanding railroad lines that pushed beyond the fringes of civilization into the heartless plains. What with thunderstorms, winds the likes of none man had ever witnessed before, grass too tall for a man to see over, wild beasts of every sort and the cursed savages, a poor soul hadn't any control over his life. What he should have done, Sean considered, which he did almost daily, was to have joined the Army. Ah, now, there was the life.

At least so it seemed to one condemned to endure the elements and unrelenting labor for the likes of the Platte River and Pacific Railroad. Why, the Union

Pacific already had a line completed beyond Promontory Summit in Utah, where it joined Mr. Stanford's Central Pacific. What need another transcontinental railroad only a couple of hundred miles north. Certainly not with the Northern Pacific completed to beyond the Cascade Mountains. That splendid gentleman, Sterling Philliphant's PR and PR actually shared common yards in Omaha with the UP. His not to reason why, Sean relented as he accepted a dipper of water from the bucket borne by a sweet-faced boy of twelve or so.

"Thank you, Timmy me lad. 'Twas sorely needed."

"You're welcome, Sean," the freckle-decorated youngster piped.

Sean studied the child's smooth features over the rim of the ladle. "Tell me," he said after a long gulp, "why is it that water boys an' cooks' helpers seem to grow younger and younger each year, while swampers an' track dressers seem to grow older?"

Timmy shrugged. "How do I know, Sean? I runned away from a drunken father in Omaha after me mother died, bless her soul. This is my first time on the railroad."

"Ah, sure an' ye'll come to love it, lad," Sean declared, dusting his palms together.

Timmy bobbed his head in uncertain agreement. Then he paused, frowning, big blue eyes staring off into the distance, perpendicular to the tracks. Sean sensed his puzzlement.

"What is it, boy?"

"I'm not sure. Sounds like a lot of hoofbeats. But . . . there's nobody out here, is there?"

" 'Cept fer the Injuns," Sean reminded the youngster. Then his eyes widened at sight of a long dust cloud in the direction Timmy had indicated. "Jesus, Mary an' Joseph! I should never have said that word. Sure an'

11

I've done conjured up the very devils themselves."

Sean turned excitedly, waving his arms. "Injuns! We's bein' attacked by the red savages!"

Startled expressions on their faces, men dropped their tools and began to run toward the triple decker dormitory cars. A tall, muscular man, dressed in quality trousers, a white shirt and vest waved his arms, directing the workers toward the strong car.

"This way, men!" he shouted. "There's rifles for all in the armory. Hurry."

A long line of warriors could be seen now, racing their ponies toward the tracks. Thin yips and howls came from their lips and they brandished an assortment of weapons that would chill the stoutest hearts. The flanks dropped back slightly, so that the charge took on an inverted crescent shape. By then, less than two hundred yards separated the Cheyennes from the work train. Several railroaders, closer to the mobile headquarters, reached the open door of the express car. They clutched eagerly at the collection of firearms produced by the paymaster.

"Take cover men," the chief construction engineer, Brendon Llewellyn, directed.

Several armed gandy dancers knelt behind stacks of creosoted ties and quickly laid out their ammunition. Others ducked under the protection of the rail cars. A few dropped behind the natural parapet formed by the track ballast and sighted on the pell mell assault.

"Shoot, damnit!" Llewellyn shouted. "Shoot at them."

"We don't know if they're peaceful or not," one older hand remarked.

"Sure an' they don't look as though they've come for Sunday tea," Sean O'Casey quipped back.

A ripple of shots and cloud of arrows came from the Cheyennes, to verify Sean's observation. At once, the bandy-legged O'Casey took aim on one warrior and squeezed the trigger. A belch of smoke obscured his view.

When the range had closed sufficiently, Spotted Horse signaled for his followers to open fire. They loosed a shower of wavering projectiles, the fletchings decorated with yellow stripes, half the shafts painted red. Several rifles fired also. The brass tacks that decorated the stock of Spotted Horse's '68 Winchester Yellow Boy glittered in the sun as he brought it to his shoulder.

Before he fired, puffs of smoke appeared from among the whites. To Spotted Horse's left, a man howled when a slug ripped along the outside of his thigh. Another warrior bit off a cry of pain and clutched at his side. Only fifty yards separated the charging Cheyennes from the disorganized railroaders. Spotted Horse rose in the wooden stirrups of his war saddle and fired at the defenders.

A smile of satisfaction illuminated his features as one of the *nia'tha* dropped his rifle and fell back, a hand gripping his wounded shoulder. Spotted Horse waved his Winchester in a signal to the right flank. Obedient to his will, the warriors lashed their ponies and surged forward, to sweep down perpendicular to the defenders.

"Ride through them!" he yelled in encouragement.

Arrows thudded into the wooden sides of the rail cars. Another white man cried out and pitched forward, a flint-tipped shaft transfixing his upper right arm. The flankers swarmed among them at that point and the railroad men broke in panic, running for the dubious shelter of their dormitory cars.

"Fire! Bring fire to use on the iron road," Spotted

Horse shouted.

Sean O'Casey saw little Timmy Pruett staring glassy-eyed at the swarming Indians, exposed and vulnerable to the shower of missiles pelting into the railroad camp. Sean broke from cover and scooped the boy up in one muscular arm, while he made a dash for the thick walled express car. No paper-thin bunk house for him.

When he reached his goal, Sean threw Timmy inside, then joined him. Adroitly, the paymaster drew the door closed to a small crack. Sean lay on his belly, firing methodically, while the clerk stood over him, blazing away with a long-barreled Wadsworth ten gauge shotgun.

"A-are they gonna kill us all, Sean?" Timmy inquired.

"Not if me an' the boys can help it," Sean answered confidently. "Ouch, the heathen devils. Would ye look at that?"

"What is it?"

"They've brought up burnin' brands. Settin' fire to the tie stacks they are. Will they be usin' 'em on the cars next?"

Tears formed in Timmy's eyes. "We'd die for sure, then, wouldn't we?"

"Bless me, lad, have ye got yer heart so set on goin' ta yer final reward that ye'll not do a thing to prevent it?"

"N-no, Sean. Only . . . what can I do?"

"Bring me another box o' them ca'tridges for a start. Then take up a rifle of yer own."

Spotted Horse rode in close among his milling braves. Two of them chivvied a frightened white man

14

toward the rolling lodges. From time to time, they would bump him with the broad chests of their ponies and send the terrified fellow sprawling. Then they would stop, to laugh and slap their bare thighs.

"Here," he called to two other of his followers. "Use your ropes."

Pointing with his rifle barrel, Spotted Horse indicated the bare, unsecured ends of the iron bands. Braided rawhide ropes snaked out and the loops closed over the offending metal strips. More Cheyennes added their lariats until half a dozen horses strained their rear flanks against the shiny rails. Slowly at first, the thick steel began to move. Then spikes came free with tortured shrieks and a distinct bow formed in each, as the forward tips bent backward.

"More! More!" Spotted Horse demanded. "Pull harder."

With a loud, bell-like tone, the bolts in the fish plates broke under tremendous pressure and sent the front rails flying across the prairie. Only skillful handling of ponies prevented injury to the warriors who had ripped out the hated ribbons of steel. Quickly they recovered their ropes and returned to try again.

A concentrated flurry of shots from the work train drove them away.

"We got 'em runnin!" Sean O'Casey shouted jubilantly.

"Yep," the paymaster agreed. "But for how long? Injuns have a habit of returnin'."

"Ain't nobody been killed yet," Timmy offered in a quiet voice. "Did you notice that, Sean?"

"We've got some wounded and so've they," the wiry gandy dancer responded.

"Still say they'll come back," Isaac Bingham, the

15

paymaster clerk predicted.

A shrill shout rallied the milling warriors and they galloped off after the ones routed from destruction of the rails. In their wake, scattered shots sounded, then silence, save for the crackling of fires.

"Are we gonna get out?" Timmy inquired.

"Not if you want to keep your hair, lad," Bingham advised. "You'll see, they ain't through with us yet."

Men began to stir outside the cars. "Get those fires out," Brendon Llewellyn shouted.

A bucket brigade formed, while Sean remained prone on the floor of the express car. Minutes passed, with water hissing into steam as the workmen vanquished the flames. Faintly, over the closer sounds, Sean heard a rhythmic drumming. He pushed upward to arm's length. Near the crest of the ridge, dust boiled up.

"B'God, they're comin' back!" he shouted.

Immediately the railroaders dove behind convenient cover. The chief construction engineer grabbed at a man running close by.

"Get a horse and ride back down the track to the telegraph," he told Big Mike Malloy, one of the track crew foremen. "Contact the Army and tell 'em what's happened. Say it's the Cheyenne who attacked. Ask for help. Fast as they can come. Put the message over my name."

"Sure, Mister Llewellyn. Only . . . what about these Injuns?"

"Leave them to us. Now, hurry."

Malloy barely had time to saddle a nervous mount and spur off along the right-of-way before the Cheyenne topped the ridge and streamed down toward the railhead. War cries shivered the air and random shots sounded dully behind the fleeing foreman.

Mike Malloy had become a small speck in the

distance when the hostiles dashed through the railroad camp, firing at the cars and once more starting fires. The Cheyenne didn't linger, though. With whoops of triumph, many bearing away tools and surveying instruments as trophies of battle, they disappeared over the rise and out of sight.

Chapter 2

Eli Holten, Chief Scout for the 12th U.S. Cavalry, couldn't believe his great good fortune. First to receive a semi-vacation by escorting a supply column to Department Headquarters in far off St. Paul, Minnesota. Then by encountering the most beautiful young woman he had seen in a long time.

Beth Chambers had a radiantly glowing complexion. A sweet smile, nicely spaced, clear blue eyes and shimmering locks of golden hair. Demure, petite, almost shy, she possessed all the refined social graces, a wondrous body and a secret abandon that made her the epitome of everything men vowed to be willing to die for. Best of all, she had chosen to reveal these womanly arts to Eli Holten.

Not that Eli had been the least reticent in pursuing her. Their introduction had come the day following the arrival of the supply train. Horses and draft mules had been left at Pierre and the quartermaster detail had boarded a train for the trip along a spur line of the Union Pacific to the junction with the St. Paul, Minneapolis and Manitoba Railroad. Heavy equipment, including four cannon, with carriages and caissons, would be freighted by rail to Dakota Territory, then off-loaded at Pierre and dragged over the scanty trails to Fort Rawlins. General Frank Corrington had suggested Eli accompany the soldiers as a friendly gesture to the scout.

What an idea that had been, Eli reflected later. He had rounded a corner of the boardwalk to nearly knock Beth Chambers onto her amply bustled posterior. A little squeak of surprise had escaped her and he reached out instinctively to steady the tottering young woman.

"I beg your pardon," Eli blurted.

"Oh! My, y-you startled me. I'm afraid I must have been day-dreaming."

"The fault was entirely mine. I cut the corner too short."

Then Eli got a look at the object of his discomfort. Had he lacked the plainsman's stoic manner, his jaw would have sagged. Such incredible beauty, for one so young, in such a nicely proportioned body. He felt the warm glow of a freshly kindled fire spreading through his rangy six-foot-plus frame. He swept the light tan, broad-brimmed hat from his head and placed it over his heart.

"May I introduce myself. I'm Eli Holten, a civilian contact scout for the Department of Dakota. I'm from Fort Rawlins."

"I'm Beth Chambers, from Saint Paul. I'm pleased to meet you, Mister Holten, though the circumstances could have been less violent." A tiny tinkle of laughter escaped her.

"Allow me to make amends by inviting you to take a cup of coffee with me."

A brief frown creased Beth's brow. "Tea, Mister Holten. I think tea would be better. We can have some little cakes with it. Over there, at the hotel."

"I'm delighted by your suggestion. And, please, call

19

me Eli."

Once they had been seated in the dining room of the lavish establishment, Beth folded her hands primly together on the edge of the table. She sat across from Eli, in a small alcove. White napery set off the dark wood tables, while heavy velvet drapes in a rich burgundy color shut out the harsh rays of the sun. The soft murmur of conversation through the room added a lazy background.

"Well, then, Eli. Now that you have me here, what do you intend to do?"

If she had any idea of what that might be, Eli thought to himself, she'd run screaming. Particularly since she could hardly be more than eighteen, maybe younger. He masked his reflection with a flicker of smile. A conscious effort softened his gray eyes.

"If I hadn't come here on business and been forced to leave in but a few days, I would ardently woo you, Beth."

This time, Beth's laughter came full-bodied and ringing with delight. "How marvelously direct and bold of you, Eli. Forgive my equal candor when I say that I would find that prospect pleasant to contemplate."

Her own evaluation of this tall, broad-shouldered, ruggedly handsome man had not found him lacking. Sun-browned and weather burnished, he maintained a youthful appearance, despite the squint creases at the corners of his eyes. No doubt he was what he claimed to be, or at least a frontiersman of some sort. A waiter arrived to spare Eli's discomfort.

"Uh, we'd like tea," Eli advised the menial. "Also some pastries to go with it."

"We have a cart you may make a selection from, sir," the soft-spoken waiter offered.

"That'll do fine." Eli paused while the white-shirted

server departed with their order. Then he reached out impulsively and placed one large, hard hand over her small, fragile ones.

"Beth, our meeting may have been a rough one, but it had to be a gift from Fate. You're a stunningly beautiful young woman. I have the misfortune of being here for only a short time. While I am, I would like to make the most of it. Will you have dinner with me tonight?"

Beth's eyes widened. She exposed white teeth, their perfection marred only by a small gap between the upper middle pair. Her nose wrinkled a moment. She appeared to be considering a matter of utmost importance.

"Yes. I'd like that, Eli. What time?"

"Seven o'clock? That's late dining for me. Out on the prairie most folks go to bed at sundown."

"Seven will be fine. Tell me, what brings you to Saint Paul?"

"A supply detail I'm scouting for. Or at least, I'll be doing my job once we get off the railroad at Pierre."

Their tea arrived, along with a tempting array of sweets on an elegant cart. They made their selections and Eli went on explaining about his duties for the Army. All the while, a part of his mind dwelt on the promise of their next meeting.

They ate that evening in the same hotel. According to Beth it was the best in town. Afterward they strolled the streets. Beth talked about her life in Saint Paul, her parents and the beer brewery her father owned. Eli regaled her with tales of frontier life. They paused for a while to listen to a band concert in the park, then Eli walked her home.

Beth gave him a chaste little kiss on the cheek. "I've

21

had a wonderful evening, Eli."

"Will I see you tomorrow?"

"Yes," Beth replied with eagerness. "What time?"

"I'd like to occupy every minute of your day."

"You . . . can, if that's what you wish."

Eli embraced her ardently and kissed her on the lips. For a moment, Beth struggled in his grasp, then she returned the buss with fervor and her arms entwined around his neck. She pressed her body firmly against his and thrilled at the growing presence of his rising manhood. At last they parted.

"I-I can prepare a picnic lunch. We could hire a boat and go out on the river. The Upper Mississippi is beautiful this time of year. And there are some small islands we can visit."

"Can we be alone there?" Eli queried eagerly.

A slow smile bloomed on Beth's face. "If you want, Eli."

"Oh, I *want* very much. Tomorrow, then, Beth?"

"Come early, dear Eli."

They took a high-sided row boat from the municipal dock. Beth had prepared a sumptuous meal. Thin slices of chicken breast lay in a sweetened vinegar marinade. She provided a roast duckling, also, and freshly made head cheese, along with a block of cheddar, a creamy brie and an assortment of fruit. A tingling hard cider complemented the repast. Eli wondered, if his plans went right, how they would eat all that. In only a few minutes of rowing, they rounded a bend and the bustling city disappeared from view.

"I'll never tire of admiring you, Beth," the scout breathed softly, shipping the oars to drift with the current.

"Why, thank you, kind sir. I dote on compliments."

Beth touched finger tips to her lips and leaned forward to place them on his. When she did, her amply filled decolletage opened wide to reveal the creamy, rounded contents. Eli swallowed with difficulty and tried to break his gaze away. Grinning foolishly, he realized that unless he received a more delightful distraction he would fail in his endeavor. Beth noticed the focus of his attention and cast her face upward to peruse his countenance.

"Ha-how far to the island?"

"Only a little way now," Beth answered.

Beth didn't resist when Eli reached out to draw her forward from the stern seat to sit on the center thwart beside him. She nuzzled up against him, making little murmuring sounds of contentment. Eli put a long, hard-muscled arm around her shoulder.

A polished brass sun turned the day into a halo glow of happiness for the pair. Eli remembered little of the journey to the island, nor of their noontime picnic. He might as well have eaten sawdust. All he could see, taste or feel was Beth. After the meal, they kissed under a large willow. Mounting ardor made them both breathless. One fiery union of lips led to another. Passion burned ravagingly within the scout's breast.

Equal desire inflamed Beth. Shyly at first, her hands began to explore Eli's massive figure. She felt of his chest and broad shoulders, the ample strength of his arms. Then she worked lower, while Eli industriously teased the sensitive nipples of her firm breasts, massaging them through the heavy cloth of her dress. Eli's tongue probed her teeth, which opened welcomingly, to give him access to the sweetness of her young mouth. Beth's questing fingers traveled the hard lines of muscle that ridged Eli's stomach and worked lower until she encircled the rigid bulk of his maleness.

Eli groaned and kissed her harder. Fascinated by the

swiftness of their growing desire, Beth wondered at it all. She hadn't expected it, planned for it, though she had to admit she had secretly desired this very thing. Oh, what a wondrous endowment he possessed. Not burdened with an excess of experience, still she thought it to be all any woman could ever want.

For Beth, experimentation had begun early. She had started self-examination and stimulation at seven. A year later, she had shared her discoveries with her sister. At nine, she'd introduced the wonderful sensations to her closest friend. Then, at twelve, she had her first exposure to boys. She and Bobby made love hurriedly and furtively. The relatively painless loss of her maidenhead and her second piercing, less than a half hour later, had convinced her that it had been the most wonderful experience of her entire life. She and the sweet, gentle boy who had deflowered her improved their technique and their endurance over the next year and a half. Then he had moved away. She mourned his loss tragically and in secret.

More than six months passed before she once more knew the vitality of a male's desire. It inflamed her. She thought herself a shameless wanton. Yet she could do nothing to bring an end to their affair. Not until after six months, when her family moved to a distant and more affluent neighborhood. Since that time, there had been but one other. Now, at seventeen, she wondered what her future might hold, and hoped it would be a *lot* of Eli Holten. Their ardor fanned to an inferno, the embrace ended.

"I . . . oh, my . . . I'm feeling faint, Eli," Beth said and suddenly blushed. She realized she still held onto his throbbing organ. She could feel its pulses through the tight weave of his whipcord trousers. Quickly she let go.

"I . . . I'm not exactly a faint-hearted maiden. I, uh,

lost that status five years ago."

"I, uh, sort of noticed that," Eli answered dryly.

"All the same, this is-isn't the way I visualized this afternoon to go."

"And so, like a moment ago, you want to let go fast and end it all?"

Eli's words stung Beth. Water filled her eyes. Swiftly, Eli bent down and kissed away her tears.

"It's all right, Beth. It's all right. We still have plenty of time together."

"Such as when?"

"Perhaps tonight, after dinner. It's obvious that we have a mutual longing and it's foolish, considering neither of us are innocent children, to deny it. When the time is right, dearest Beth, we'll accomplish what we set out to do."

"You're . . . so darned sure of yourself."

"Of us, Beth. *Of us*. Now, come, I'll help you with the picnic things and we can start back."

"Oh, I wish this moment would never end."

Roguish humor lighted Eli's gray eyes and he brushed a long lock of golden hair off his forehead. "It doesn't have to, you know."

"Oh . . . oh-oh, *men!*"

"Not 'men,' Beth. This particular man. I know what I want and you've told me what you desire. There's no reason we should deprive ourselves. Am I right?"

"Right, darling Eli. Only it has come on so fast. Let's wait for the future. See what tonight brings."

"I shall do so with bated breath."

"You're teasing," Beth accused.

"No. Definitely not that. I'm deadly, uh, no, make that amorously serious. Hurry now. It'll be a long, hard row back."

Eli and Beth dined on a pair of squab, a succulent venison roast and a variety of squash dishes. Afterward, they went to Eli's room and made long, slow, delightful love. When three delirious plunges into eroticism had sated them, Beth proposed another boat venture the next day, to which Eli eagerly agreed.

He met her at ten-thirty, outside the white picket fence that gave access to the municipal dock. At first she seemed a bit shy and reticent. Eli dismissed it as a facet of her youth. Once more the delightful girl had brought along a magnificent feast.

"There's cucumber and beet pickles, boiled eggs, a broiled hare, smoked sausages and half a plum pie," she proudly told him. "All prepared by my own hands. I chased cook and his helpers out of the kitchen. Let's hurry. I can hardly wait."

Her return of enthusiasm encouraged Eli. When they obtained another high-sided skiff, he suggested that he do the hard work first and row upstream, then they could drift back down. Beth agreed. Once away from the city, the farmland vista opened wide. Bees and butterflies worked industriously, jealous of the little time they had left before the ravages of winter. Birds sang. Tall stalks of corn, brown and dry now in the last days before harvest, rattled in a sweet, earthy breeze like a dozen Sioux shamans. Eli's chest swelled with contentment as he plied the oars.

"Once we get past the prying eyes of the local farmers, I'm going to tie this boat up to a tree limb and we're going to have an onboard lunch. Then I'm going to make wild, passionate love with you, right here in the bottom of the boat," Eli announced.

For an instant, Beth looked startled, then produced a warm, inviting smile. "Oh, Eli. I've never dreamed of such a romantic encounter. Yes, let's do it like that."

The last of the hard cider disappeared in frugal sips.

Beth dabbed at her mouth with a white linen napkin and began assembling the remainders in the large wicker hamper she had brought, the same one that had been along the previous day. Her task completed, Beth leaned forward and kissed Eli soundly on the lips.

"Ummm. You taste nice. Like good wine and sweet venison."

"You're definitely on the appetizing side, yourself," Eli observed.

In that moment, their mutual need seized them and they embraced roughly, bodies clinging, writhing against the unwanted confinement of clothing. Beth moaned. Her hand slid down Eli's back and around his waist. Fingers trailed delicately across his thigh and then closed over his rising manhood. Beth squeezed and began to stroke. Eli started to fumble with the buttons of her dress.

"Be quick, beloved," Beth gasped as she plucked at the opening to Eli's trousers.

In moments, their clothing lay in a welter over the seats of the boat. Beth gasped at the size of Eli's penis, as though she had not seen, held, kissed and been penetrated by it the night before.

Eli nestled her in his arms and began kissing her face, neck and breasts. His hands made busy with stimulating the many erotic spots on her flushed, creamy skin. Beth began languidly stroking Eli's pulsating maleness, thrilling at its appearance and wonderful texture. Without need of direction, she bent forward and took the ruby tip through the portal of her lips.

Her tongue sent shivers of rapture through Eli's body. Gradually, Beth worked deeper on his solid lance.

"Aaah. Beth, Beth. You're a delight."

Beth worked harder, drawing more pleasure from

27

him. The boat rocked to the rhythm of her bobbing head. Eli's legs straightened and he felt his pulse increase. His belly tightened. The world seemed to swim around him. Falling leaves made mystic patterns in the air. Little chills of ecstasy rippled her skin. Eli began to thrust with his hips, matching her actions to heighten the enjoyment of each. Skillfully she prolonged the ultimate, exhibiting considerable knowledge in how to avoid the crescendo until they both became wracked by spasms of unbearable sensation. Then, with selfless determination, the lovely young woman brought him raging to a conclusion.

"A boat's a wonderful place to make love," she declared a short while later.

Her fingers idly toyed with Eli's semi-relaxed organ. As she persisted, it began to quickly rise to new life.

"You're a wonderful person to be with in a boat like this. Thank you for sharing your goodness."

"You've made me so happy, I should be thanking you."

"Humm. C'mere, you lovely thing. Let's see what new distraction we can devise."

"Oh, Eli. Fulfill my wildest wishes. Spear me with that remarkable device so that I can always know that at least for a while, I was a complete woman."

"It's you who complete me," Eli protested as he rose to his knees and maneuvered precariously in the wobbly boat.

Beth spread wide her legs and Eli lowered himself until he felt the thrilling contact of his rigid member with the dew-moist petals of her swollen mound. Sparsely furred, it gave him even greater reward by its heat and tight dimensions. With tender care and infinite patience, Eli drove into the silken purse that presented itself for enriching. As he slid into her quivering passage, he reached out with one hand and untied the knot that held them to the bank.

Floating away on the current, they whirled off into a world all their own.

Chapter 3

Long, red shafts of dying sunlight streamed through the curtains to illuminate Eli Holten's hotel room. After three days and nights of tender loving, his delightful sojurn in St. Paul had nearly ended. In the morning, the military supplies would be loaded on rail cars and shortly after noon the next day, the supply detail would depart for Pierre, Dakota Territory and the long, hard journey to Fort Rawlins. For once in his life, itchy feet of a frontiersman notwithstanding, Eli hated to go.

Beth Chambers possessed an unflagging sexual energy that had nearly drained the scout. Yet, he eagerly anticipated every trip to that fountain of delights. For tonight, he had been promised a special adventure.

"A double portion," Beth had told him archly.

Holten wondered what that could be. So far their amorous exchanges had brought mutual exhaustion at each conclusion. How could she offer more? A soft knock presaged an answer to his question.

Eli crossed the room in rapid strides. The innate caution of a Westerner prevented him from throwing wide the door. Rather, he held his Remington .44 in one hand and stood to the side of the portal. In a low voice he inquired the identity of his visitor.

"It's Beth," came the reply.

Even then, Eli opened the door only a crack, to peer out. Satisfied, he flung the thin wooden panel wide. And stopped in astonishment, mouth opening to speak when no words would form.

"Hello, Eli, dear. I promised you double and you've got it. May we come in?"

"Uh . . . er, of course." Eli stepped back and ushered two divinely lovely young women into his room.

Blithely, Beth chattered away, oblivious to Eli's amazement. "This is my sister, Bonny. But, of course, you've met her before."

"I . . . uh, have?"

"Sure you have," Bonny cooed as she took an impulsive step toward the scout. "Beth and I have been, er, trading off. Over the past few days, you've made love to both of us in turn."

"Twins," Eli forced out, his head swimming.

Both Chambers girls replied with titters of laughter. "Absolutely identical," Beth told him. "You don't think one of us could have handled so much loving by herself, do you?"

"Then, uh, that is, you've been . . . and I . . . w-what about tonight."

"You get . . ." Bonny began.

"To have us . . ." Beth added.

"Together," they completed in chorus.

Holten's knees felt weak. He didn't know exactly what to make of this. *Always do your best.* That maxim, learned from the old mountain man who had taught Eli much of his woodscraft long years ago, rang in his mind. He flushed, smiled and gestured toward a small table, set with a light supper.

"I thought we'd like a little something to eat," Eli began lamely.

"You know what *I* like to eat," Bonny blurted.

"Me, too," Beth quickly concurred.

31

Eli flushed again. Yes, he definitely *knew*. "Well, uh, we really should. Keep up our strength, so to speak?"

"You're a dear, Eli," said Beth, who kissed him on his right cheek.

"Yes, you are," agreed Bonny, who kissed him on his left.

The trio dabbled over the food. Closeness, novelty and the conversation built their individual excitement. After a few bites of cold roast beef, Eli invited an explanation.

"Tell me about this sharing idea of yours."

"It started a long time ago," Beth took up the tale. "I learned how to pleasure myself when I was seven. Within a year, I'd learned it was a lot more fun to share pleasure with my sister," Beth admitted without a trace of embarrassment.

"We'd always been close," Bonny began. "So, once Beth had mastered the way to do it, she couldn't wait to share with me. When you're eight, it's absolutely wonderful."

"It still is," Beth added impishly. "Why don't we show Eli?"

Beth began to unfasten the buttons of her blouse, only to stop at Bonny's words. "We can do that later. I'm sure Eli would like to hear more."

"Yes. I'm fascinated." Stirred by this unconventional revelation, the scout's ample organ had begun to stiffen. This passionate pair aroused him now in a manner he'd not experienced before.

"Well," Beth continued, "we found we could almost feel what each other experienced. Made it better than with anyone else. The next year we started taking turns with our best friend, Trudy Simms. Being girls, we'd been told all the awful things about boys and why we had to stay away from them. Still, we had these *feelings*, if you know what I mean. Like an itch that had to be scratched from time to time or a person would go crazy. So, being warned off boys, we just naturally had to take care of it among ourselves."

"Works the same with boys," Bonny told her sister. "Remember Tommy Barnes in eighth grade? He was the second boy I ever did anything with. I shared him with Beth, too, Eli. Real shy and nervous the first time. He didn't know how to go about it. So I got him up and rarin' to go and . . . nature took over. Afterward, he told me how he and his friends lolly-gagged together to ease the pressure. They'd been told they'd burn in Gehenna if they ever touched a girl's private parts, yet they burned on earth with the need to relieve their own itches. Why is it that so many folks think that something that is so much fun has to be evil?"

"Uh . . . you've got me there," Eli replied, uncomfortable with his rising hunger.

"Beth was first," Bonny returned to the narrative. "About a month after we turned twelve, it was. A real nice boy, a year older than us, who lived next door."

"Like most boys his age, he'd never had any real experience. He fumbled and shook and jerked around so he nearly couldn't do it. We found a way, though. It was the most wonderful time in my entire life. After Bobby and I figured out about three ways to give each other pleasure, Bonny and I decided to switch off on him, like we had with Trudy."

Both young lovelies twittered with laughter. "Poor Bobby. He never knew we took turns after that. It became so much fun for us, that we've done it that way ever since."

"How is it you decided to let me in on your secret?" Eli pondered.

"You're . . . different, somehow. It would have been like cheating not to let you know. And you're strong as a bull. We knew you could take care of us both at once

33

and we could give you something you'd maybe never had before."

"Uh . . . at least not with twins."

"So you see, dear Eli," Beth sparkled. "This will be a first for all of us."

In a graceful, feline move, she slid from her chair and curled her legs under her beside Eli. Her small, delicate hand began to caress the inside of his thigh. A raging cataract exploded through the scout's system. Bonny joined her sister on the floor, at Eli's opposite side and pursued the same ministration. With their free hands, they began to unfasten and remove his trousers. Gleefully, Eli began a little exploration of his own.

Carefully he slid his hands into open bodices. With thumb and forefinger, to left and right, he began to tease a nipple on each beautiful creature. Eli used his feet to move the table away from them. Coolness surrounded his groin when the twins managed to pull away his whipcords and longjohns.

"The boots," he instructed. "Get my boots off."

Bonny set to that, while Beth encircled the thick bulk of his long, smooth shaft. In less than a minute, her sister joined her. Together they began to stroke him. Eli marveled at this wondrous treasure. As though by unspoken agreement, Beth and Bonny leaned forward.

Two pair of lips, two tongues began to nibble and taste at the hot flesh of his phallus. Two hands clung to him. Transported, filled with a strange, new delight, Eli leaned back and sighed heavily.

With matched eagerness, the twins went noisily about their task. Gratitude lacked strength for the sensation their efforts engendered in the scout. He tingled and twitched and sought to make the most intimate contact with each of these magnificent women. Experience forewarned them when to cease and change the rules of the game.

"Can we get in bed now?" Beth asked in a little girl voice.

"Can't think of anything I'd like more," Eli quipped.

Swiftly, the twins rose and disrobed. They pulled pins from their hair and let the long tresses fall free. Even naked, Eli could not tell them apart. He went to the large, brass-framed bed and sprawled lengthwise on it, back to the mattress. His elongated shaft rose triumphantly from a thatch of curly, dark hair. Hand-in-hand, his wonderful pair hurried to join him.

Eli reached out and took Beth—or was it Bonny?—by the inviting flare of her hips and drew her atop him. Smiling sweetly, the lovely girl straddled Eli's waist and lowered herself onto his massive device. Ecstasy exploded in both their heads as her plunge drove a great portion of his pillar deep within her welcoming purse. Her sister recognized what she must do and quickly joined them on the sheets.

Inverted, she lowered her musk-sweet cleft over Eli's face while her tongue flicked out to lave the remaining increment of his turgid maleness. Heady with rapture, the trip spun off into oblivion.

The infinite variety the lusty threesome could invent lasted long into the night. Never stinting, Eli delivered pleasure for every pleasure he gained. They stopped once in a while to refresh with chilled champagne and almond iced cakes. Not for long, though. The bed always invited a return to herculean efforts and olympian rewards.

At one point, Eli rested while Beth and Bonny put on an invigorating demonstration of the tender ways of love they had evolved with each other. It fired the scout to new heights. Their *menage a trois* continued until a pale light entered the room.

"It must be nearly dawn," Beth gasped when the realization came to her.

"There's still time for one more," Bonny urged.

"The spirit's willing, but the flesh is, ah, sore," Eli protested.

"Oh, our poor, poor dear," the twin consoled.

Eli felt a familiar stirring. "Well, perhaps . . . just a . . . little more?"

A knock interrupted a promising new arrangement of the aroused trio.

"Desk clerk. There's a telegram for Mister Eli Holten."

"Damn," Eli exploded. "Be right there."

He rose from his bed of joys and slid into his trousers. At the portal, he opened it a crack to receive the message. The desk clerk accepted the quarter tip and gave Eli a conspiratorial wink.

"Dirty old bastard," Eli growled. He opened the yellow form and groaned.

"What is it?" Beth inquired.

"Bad news. I'm to take the morning train, ahead of the supply detail, change in Omaha and make haste to Pierre. Then on to Fort Rawlins."

"Oh, how awful," Bonny added her disappointment. "Is it something important?"

"Indian trouble," the scout told her flatly.

Amid the wails and lamentations of the delightfully horny twins, Eli Holten dressed, packed his single bag and departed for the railroad depot.

Disappearing with the sun, the unusually early frost melted away from the browned grass around the railhead. The triangle clanged stridently and summoned men forth from the dormitory cars to stand in line for their grub. Steam smogged the windows of the kitchen car and the aroma of coffee, gravy and fresh-baked biscuits hung heavily in the air. Sean O'Casey yawned prodigiously and stretched himself, then scratched at his faded red longjohns. Beside him, eyes aglow with hero worship, Timmy Pruett imitated the gandy dancer. They donned trousers, slid on their low-top boots, shrugged into woolen jackets and started for the mess line. Over the usual morning sounds, Sean heard a distinctly familiar rumble.

A quick look to the west told him the worst. "Ja-zas! Here they come again!"

Shouts of alarm rose from the workmen when they recognized the feathers and lances of the charging war party. Breakfast forgotten, they scurried to obtain weapons and take positions to defend themselves. Excited and scared, the engineer on the locomotive began to hoot the whistle in a long series of shorts. Once more, Sean and Timmy opted for the express car.

"Thick walls," Sean explained as though a new concept. "Helps keep the bullets out."

Firing began almost at once. Before it seemed possible, the Cheyennes swarmed down onto the construction site. A powder monkey reared up and backward, a lance point in his right shoulder. His shrieks of agony went lost in the general turmoil. The railroaders began to grow more accurate in their fire. Two warriors flew from their saddles. Another clutched a wounded biceps. Arrows hummed in morbid chorus.

"Keep down, Timmy me lad," Sean urged from the floor of the express car.

"Can't," the boy grunted. "Gotta get you some bullets."

"Na-na, lad. Be fer keepin' yer'sel' alive."

Slugs thudded into the door of the coach. Timmy

37

raised a light shotgun and fired one barrel. The recoil sat him on his round bottom. A loud, ululating cry rose from around the water tower. Sean and Timmy smelled smoke.

"Saints preserve us. They've found a way to set fire to the water tank."

Another hoot, authoritative and final sounded.

In a chorus of yelps and wails, the Cheyenne grouped up and swirled away through the clouds of dust and powder smoke. For the time being, at least, the attack had ended.

Chapter 4

Uh-oh. Things had to be really bad.

Frank Corrington's cigar box sat open, near the front edge of his desk and the brandy decanter held a prominent place on the rosewood sideboard. Two company commanders of the 12th Cavalry, Dave Roberts and Winfield Stone, sat with upright postures on a pair of straight-back chairs, crystal glasses in their left hands. Early morning sunlight streamed through the windows of the commanding general's office at Fort Rawlins, Dakota Territory. From outside came the barks of non-commissioned officers conducting dismounted drill. In the far distance, Eli Holten imagined he could hear the cheery trill of meadowlarks. What cause did they have to be happy?

"You made good time, Eli," General Corrington remarked as he rose and extended a hand to shake that of the scout.

"Railroads are the wonder of the age, General," Eli replied dryly.

"*That* remains to be seen. Now, let's get down to cases. Captain Roberts and Lieutenant Stone are here for the same reason you are. As it is, Eli, I don't know how to go about telling you this."

"Then why not forego the necessity?"

Frank Corrington scowled. Then he waved his hand

toward the cigar box. "Take one, Eli. And I'll pour you some brandy. We're a bit ahead of you as it is."

"Get to the point, Frank."

"Nice to have someone who's all business around this place. All right, since you insist. The, ah, Cheyenne are raiding in Dakota Territory. Not out on the fringes, but within seventy miles of Fort Rawlins. Along a new railroad right-of-way. Have you heard of the Platte River and Pacific Railroad?"

While Eli considered the question, Corrington stood and crossed to the sideboard. Mounted animal heads and cured hides decorated two paneled walls of the office, while a pair of windows, with a pot-bellied stove between, occupied the one facing onto the parade ground. The third contained the general's only concession to the niceties of life in the East. The sideboard reached from floor to ceiling. It contained crystal glasses and decanters, thick ceramic mugs and a silver tea service. To the left, near the door, a hall tree of the same wood gleamed dully. On the right, an ornate commode held a glazed ceramic pitcher and basin, decorated with images of ancient battles. Corrington appreciated his small comforts. He poured fine liquor into a glass and handed it to his favorite scout.

"No," Eli answered while the general had his back to him. "That's a new one."

"Right. Headquarters is in Omaha. From there the main line curves northwest into the Territory. End of track is now only a few miles short of the Bad Lands. Some hot-shot promoter convinced a pack of Eastern investors that another route was needed between the Union and Northern Pacific lines. Which is what brings us here today. It's the Platte River construction crews that are being attacked by the Cheyenne."

"What brought them out of Montana?" Eli inquired. "Those who weren't shipped south to Indian Territory usually try to stay as far as possible from any white men."

"It appears that they don't want this railroad to cross their country," Dave Roberts offered. His dark blue eyes sparkled and he flashed a white, boyish grin.

"How'd the general ring you in on this, Davey?" Eli asked of his long-time friend.

Roberts ran long, artist's fingers through his nearly white blond hair. Not as tall as Holten, his slender frame held ample muscle and the youthful appearance of his face belied his thirty years. A ladies' man, every bit as much as the scout, he discreetly kept his amorous adventures from impinging on his military career. He produced his engaging smile again before answering.

"I was getting bored, Eli. Troop drill, routine patrol. I, uh, volunteered."

"*Never* volunteer. That's the cardinal rule of the military, Davey."

"Harumph! Ah, Eli, I'll not have you subverting my officers," Corrington chided. His voice held a tone of affability, though.

The friendship between Eli Holten and Dave Roberts went back a number of years. To the time, in fact, when newly promoted First Lieutenant David Roberts arrived at Fort Rawlins to take his first command of a company. A quick learner, with keen intelligence and an insight into the problems of dealing with Indians, Roberts had adapted in a surprisingly short time. The regimental commander developed a habit of calling on his most junior company commander to perform tasks that baffled officers of longer service on the frontier. Eli counseled and guided him. Considering the anti-Army sentiments of Congress in the years following the War Between the States, it came as a surprise to everyone when Dave Roberts received an increase in rank to captain, long before many senior

41

to him had been so favored. With becoming modesty, Dave Roberts attributed his success to the talents of Eli Holten.

"Gentlemen, let's get back to this business of the Cheyenne," Frank Corrington injected. "Captain Roberts and Lieutenant Stone are taking their companies into the field to provide protection for the railroad construction crew. I want you to scout for them, Eli. Also to interpret. I know, your Cheyenne is limited, but most of them speak Lakota. Your purpose is to contact the hostiles, parlay with them and . . . uh, somehow convince them to break off the fighting and return to Montana. Or go south to Oklahoma."

"A rather ambitious undertaking, Frank," Eli observed. "The last thing they want to do is go to Indian Territory. You've seen the reports regarding unrest there. Don't think these Cheyenne are any less aware of it. As to stopping their attacks on the railroad, a lot will depend on how many they are and in what mood we find them."

Corrington cleared his throat in an impatient rumble. "That's what Captain Roberts remarked also. This isn't an easy one. Far from it. However, the railroads have the right to call on the Army for protection. We have to provide it."

"How many railroaders have been killed so far?"

"That's the odd part. None that we know of. Does that sound like the Cheyenne to you, Eli?"

"No-o," the scout drawled. "Hardly what I expected. Have any Sioux warriors been identified among them?"

"No, thank God. So far it is almost as though the Sioux were unaware of what went on in their own back yard. I've communicated with Department Headquarters. It's their consensus that as long as the Sioux remain out of it, we will be spared a general uprising.

What we don't need is another Little Big Horn. Sioux, Cheyenne, Arapahoes, all joined in a common cause. The whole frontier could be ablaze, from Kansas to Canada. So, they want us to bottle up the Cheyenne before the Sioux get wind of it and come join the fun."

"You always give me the simple jobs, Frank," Eli complained with mock severity.

"That's because I know you handle them so well. Boots and Saddles after noon chow. There's some nasty looking clouds building in the northwest. No telling what might come down on us. Captain, Lieutenant, have your companies stand to at twelve-thirty. Eli, after you get your gear taken care of, will you eat with me in my quarters?"

"Might as well get whatever I can out of this."

Corrington smiled for the first time. "Mrs. O'Mara is cooking for me this week, Eli."

"Saints preserve us," Eli exclaimed in a passable Irish accent. "Will it be the corned beef and cabbage or Irish stew?"

"Roast buffalo back ribs, most likely. With creamed potatoes and onions and watermelon pickle."

Holten brightened. "Then you can count on me, General."

Unseasonable bad weather brewed on the plains. Masses of cold air swept down from Canada, bringing a biting, raw wind. In columns of fours, as long as the road lasted, the two company patrols cantered out of Fort Rawlins and into the teeth of a bitter chill. Mountainous clots of cloud swirled ominously to the front and thicker masses to the northwest. To make matters worse, Eli Holten experienced a growing discomfort.

A raw soreness irritated his throat. His nose grew

dry and the burning sensation persisted. His actual duties wouldn't begin for a good two days, after they left the established road and cut southward to the railroad. Perhaps he could shake it in that time, he considered.

"Damned inconvenient," Dave Roberts remarked. "This weather. Could make our job harder."

"Let's not borrow trouble, Davey," Eli advised. "It's too early for any long stretch of bad weather."

"All the same . . ."

"Know what you mean. We've both seen some hellers this time of the year. If you were the war chief of this Cheyenne party, what would you do if we got hit by a heavy snow?"

Roberts' pale, blond eyebrows raised in contemplation. "I'd go to ground, I suppose. Wait it out. If more came, I'd head for home."

"*Or*-dinarily, I'd do it the same way. But say you're here to stop a great evil. Something that threatened the future of the tribe more than the prolonged absence of a couple of dozen warriors? What then?"

Frequently the two friends would employ this method of inquiry to test their plainscraft. It provided distraction and often led to useful decisions that affected the outcome of a mission. Eli and Davey enjoyed the banter and the mental exercise. Now Roberts pursed his lips, wrinkled his nose and made cautious reply.

"I'd say that the Great Spirit—uh, what's the Cheyenne word for that?"

"*Heammawihio*. It means, Wise One Above."

"All right. So, *heammawihio* had ordained that the railroad be stopped and that there was no choice but to keep on until it had been."

"Good thinking!" Eli enthused. "And that's what I predict we'll be looking at, good weather or bad."

44

Three hours out from the fort, Eli developed a dry, persistent cough. It came from deep in his chest, which had grown tight and painful. His nose ran and his eyes had the red glow of a three-day drunk. The soreness in his chest intensified, as did the icy blasts of wind driving from the northwest.

"That doesn't sound good," Dave Roberts remarked after another fit of hacking subsided.

"It feels even less promising. Damned if I don't think I'm coming down with something."

"Bucking for a way to get out of this?" Dave joked.

"The idea had occurred, Davey. But I'm more worried about this weather than myself. A couple of shots of Panther Piss and some wild honey ought to cure whatever it is nagging at my innards."

"Don't count on it. From the sounds you're making, you've got a good case of something awful brewing."

"We'll make camp in an hour. There's a good creek flowing there."

"Yeah. Half way to Eagle Pass. Do you figure to ride on in during the night and wait for us at the Thunder Saloon?"

"Not a bad idea. Be better if you came along. Lottie's been asking about you."

"Me? What did I ever do to be so fondly remembered?"

"Not so fondly. Seems there's every chance you're gonna be a daddy."

Davey blanched. "Wha . . ." he managed in a strangled croak. "You mean . . . ? That, I . . . I . . . uh, got her in a family way?"

"Countin' backwards, that's how she figures it. Don't worry, though. If it was you, the little nipper'll be the perfect image of his handsome father."

"Yu-you horse's ass! Does anyone at Fort Rawlins know about this?"

45

"No. Why should they? After all, it's all between you and Lottie. Considerin' her occupation, she's hardly in a position to raise a fuss."

"You're not really that callous, Eli. I know you better."

The scout looked shamefaced a moment. "Right on that score, Davey. And I know you're not either. I already set aside a hundred dollars for the kid's up-bringing."

"You can count on me for a like amount," Davey said fervently. "With smaller sums from time to time. Me, a father," he went on wonderingly. "It kind of has a ring to it."

"Don't go countin' your chickens before they turn out tow-headed," Eli countered his friend's enthrallment. "After all, you weren't exactly the only one to, ah, take notice of Lottie."

Davey grinned impishly. "Still, it would be nice to have a boy of my own."

"It'd be nicer if I could clear up this pestiferous quinsey."

Chapter 5

A uniform gray covered the sky. Like sheets of falling glass, freezing rain lashed the troops from Fort Rawlins. Three days out on the trail to the new railroad, they had left all trappings of civilization far behind. No shelter afforded itself to them. The few trees and tall, brown grass became coated with ice, glistening in fairy-like splendor. The men of the 12th Cavalry, under command of Captain Roberts and Lieutenant Stone had no time to appreciate the beauty. Their animals and themselves likewise became encrusted with a sheen of crystals. Eli Holten had ridden ahead to seek some form of protection from the driving cold wind and relentless onslaught of sleet.

His task suffered from his physical condition. The persistent cough had become worse and he felt feverish. A turn of his head made him reel in the saddle as sudden dizziness rushed over him. He could barely swallow. Tender nodes had swollen on both sides of his throat. He was desperately sick, though he could do nothing about it. The troops depended on him. The two assistant scouts who had accompanied the column had gone on far ahead to mark the route. Eli shuddered as a particularly violent gust of frigid wind buffeted him. He'd have to find something fast. Unrelenting, the violence of nature continued and numbed by the storm, Eli's thoughts drifted back to the column's brief stop in Eagle Pass.

Lottie Palmer was sure-enough six months pregnant and showing it. She greeted Eli Holten and Davey Roberts warmly in the big main room of the Thunder Saloon.

"Eli, Davey. Am I glad to see you. C'mere and let me give you both a big smack."

She'd hugged and kissed both men, then stood back, hands on hips. Her distended belly protruded before her. For a silent moment, she gave Dave a long, calculating look.

"I, uh, see it's, er, true about . . . about . . ." Davey stammered.

"Sure as bad weather in January. 'Nother three months an' out pops the li'll one."

"Th-that soon? Is there . . . is there any chance that . . . I'm . . . ?"

Lottie, her thick brown hair swaying in sausage curls, threw back her head and chortled mightily. "Any chance? Davey, my love, there's every good chance. Not that I'm blamin' you. Risk of the business, so's to speak."

"Y-you're taking it lightly enough." The young lieutenant could not overcome his discomfort.

"Can't exactly wish it away, now can I? Besides, figgerin' it comes from you, I ain't all that fired up about bein' shut of the little bugger when he gets here."

Dave had the grace to blush. "You mean, you *want* the child?"

"Sure. Don't you?"

"I . . . uh, I never thought of it before."

"Now's a good time to start, Davey," Eli injected. "If you're going to be a father, you'd better begin thinking like one."

Davey's boyish face crinkled in concentration and the light scatter of freckles over the bridge of his nose writhed with his efforts. "Well, if that's the case, then, I

. . . well, the mother of my son has no business working in a place like this. We'll have to . . . to find better, ah, accommodations." A thought suddenly struck him. Eyes wide, his jaw gaped a moment.

"Say, we're all saying 'he' and 'him.' What if it's a girl?"

"It could be," Lottie replied. "Though I'm carryin' a might bit high for that. Best anyone can predict, it'll be a boy."

"A son of my own." A tone of prideful wonder crept into Davey's voice. "We'll name him Joseph Marcus for my brother and my Dad."

For a brief instant, Lottie's eyes narrowed. "What about my side of the family?"

"Oh, ah, I forgot. I've never named a child before. What other names would you like him to have?"

Somewhat shyly, eyes lowered, Lottie replied in a small voice. "Christopher, after my father."

"Joseph Marcus Christopher Roberts. It's settled then. I hope he'll grow up big enough to carry all that around."

"This calls for a celebration," Eli Holten declared.

"Oh, ah, one thing more," Dave interrupted.

Wild visions spun in his head of a new background and history for Lottie. No denying she was a pretty thing, with hazel eyes and thick, luxuriant sable hair. A small, inviting mouth and high cheekbones. Lots of curves in all the best places. Altogether a pleasing package. Except for her spotted past as a fallen angel, she could be acceptable in any society. Particularly the army.

"What's that, Davey?" Eli pressed.

"Uh . . . Lottie, er, this is hardly the place and all, but, uh . . . would you . . . would you consent to be my wife?"

A stunned silence held in the Thunder Saloon. All

faces turned to where the three people stood.

"My . . . my God. Did I hear you rightly, Davey? You want to marry me?"

"Yes. Oh, yes. I . . . I've never had a wife. Never tired of playing in the posies you might say. But . . . well, with a kid on the way and all. I mean, it's the right thing to do."

"The *right* thing!" Lottie snapped. "Is that the only reason? To 'make an honest woman' of me? Well, Captain David Roberts, let me tell you a thing or . . ."

"Lottie! No, Lottie. That's not it at all. It's . . . it's because . . . I . . . I love you."

Dave Roberts startled himself with that fervent declaration. Lottie began to cry. Several of her sisters in shame joined in. Then the celebration began. The next morning, when the patrol rode out of Eagle Pass, both Eli Holten and David Roberts had sore heads.

The sound of his chattering teeth broke Eli's reverie. Where? What was it? A fleeting impression hinted of finding something important. A deep draw, seen within the last few minutes. A cottonwood filled dry creek bed, high banks, an ideal shelter from the storm. Patiently, body afire with his illness, Eli turned Sonny's nose and retraced his track.

With his back to the storm, searching became easier. Ice covered Eli's hat, the saddle horn and skirt, the stirrups and the fringes of his leather trousers. It coated the stock of his Winchester and hung in icicles from his thick buffalo hide coat. A constant buzz sounded in his head. He coughed frequently, thin and weak. Without conscious passage of time, a black slash spread before him in the sleet-blanketed prairie.

He'd found the shelter so desperately sought after.

"Those eyes look like piss holes in the snow, Eli,"

Davey Roberts told the scout.

They sat beside a snapping, crackling fire of cotton-wood limbs a lean-to rigged to act as a further wind-break. The ice storm continued, a howling tempest that occasionally dipped down into the dry creek bed. Eli alternately shook with chills and burned with fever. He clasped a tin cup in his big, work-roughened hands as though it alone sustained his life. Lieutenant Winfield Stone joined them a minute later.

"From the looks of it out there, this could get worse before it gets better," Stone began their strategy talk.

"Any sign of snow?" Eli inquired.

"Not so far. Just more and more sleet. There's enough ice out there to chill all the juleps in Georgia. Do we go on or turn back?"

"That's a blunt way of putting it, Winn," Dave returned. "Can we afford to make such a loose interpretation of orders?"

"Davey's right, Winn. The way the general put it, we don't have a lot of choice in this."

"But, what about your condition, Eli? You sound like a love-sick bullfrog and your eyes look like . . ."

"Yeah. I know. Two piss holes in the snow. Frank Corrington expects us to carry out our assignment. If we don't it could get a hell of a lot worse. What I need is a big shot of wild honey and some white whiskey. Odds are, this will blow over by morning. We *have* to go on. Only a couple of days ride from here to the railhead."

"What you *need* is a few days in a warm room . . . in bed," Dave Roberts inserted. "But you're right. We have to get after these Cheyenne. Winn, Eli and I talked about this the first day out. Way we read the hostiles, they'll figure they're committed. No way to just break it off and go home until spring. Which means we have to confront them, bad weather or not.

51

If it clears, we'll move out at dawn. If not, we wait until we have all the light we can."

Frozen rain stopped falling from the sky around one o'clock in the morning. A thick, wooly overcast remained. An hour before sunup, Brian Chalmers, First Sergeant of Dave Roberts' Company D, roused the troops. The odor of coffee and frying fatback filled the creek bed. Eli Holten breathed with an audible wheeze. He looked no better than the night before.

"Flip a coin?" the scout inquired when he rose from a pile of blankets and shrugged into his heavy coat.

"It's still clouded over," Dave remarked. "Though no more sleet, thank God. I'm for putting as many miles behind us as we can. Let's go when it gets light enough to see."

"I'll put Bill Fletcher and Tommy Red Hawk out front. They can eat and leave within half an hour."

Dave gave Eli a close look. "You're startin' to worry me, Eli. You want to take a turn in one of the wagons? Stay out of the cold a bit?"

"Hell, Davey, you know I can't do that. I'll have to range back and forth between the column and our advance scouts."

"The way you look, you could fall on your ass out there on the prairie and we'd never find you. I could make it an order."

"You could try spittin' into the wind, too."

Dave shrugged and produced a small grin. "Well, I'm glad that's settled. When you get over to the grub line, stuff yourself. You're gonna need the energy."

Two hours after daylight, a light snow began to fall. Big, fat, wet flakes tumbled out of the sky, to melt as they touched bare ground. Although still cold, the wind had dropped to a light breeze. Eli Holten rode ahead to check his subordinate scouts.

"Damn this weather," Bill Fletcher told the chief scout when Eli trotted up to where he waited on his big gelding.

"Can't argue that, Bill. How far ahead is Tommy?"

"Maybe an hour. With this snow coming on, he's already looking for a place to shelter 'till the storm passes."

"Good idea. Might not hurt to shorten the march a bit more. I'm gonna ride on up and bring Tommy back. Not much around here for shelter, but the troops can pitch tents for tonight."

"There's a copse of blackjack pine over that rise," Fletcher told Eli. "Make a good windbreak and provide firewood."

"Ideal, considering. Get a start at setting it up while I find Tommy."

"Take care of yourself, Eli. You sound terrible. And your eyes . . ."

"Uh-huh. I've heard it already."

Shortly before mid-morning, Eli Holten reached the spot where Tommy Red Hawk had stopped. He had found a high cutbank to the northwest that would effectively shelter a campsite. Lodge pole pines and some scrub oak dotted a meadow formed by a shallow depression. Ideal. Only the snow fell heavier now and the distance from the starting point would keep the column from reaching this haven before late afternoon. The wind had come up also. It bit and slashed at exposed skin. Holten felt worse than he had the previous night. He clasped forearms in Dakota fashion with the half-breed Sioux scout.

"You know how to pick 'em, Tommy. A perfect spot. With this storm getting heavier, I don't think the patrol can reach this place in time, though."

"*Unkce!*" Tommy exploded, then repeated in English,

"Shit. I'm sitting here, half frozen, and smellin' a big white-out comin' from the northwest an' you have to tell me I did it all for nothin'. Why'd I ever come to work for the Army?"

"Because I asked you to. Best way for me to keep track of my adopted nephew."

"You might be *mihunka*, but I don't need a keeper."

"Oh? What about that Pawnee girl at Beaverton's trading post? She almost scalped you in the short hairs," Holten joked.

Tommy unconsciously clutched at his crotch. "Damn. You would have to bring that up. So, I got a little bit of the hots for her an' didn't think payin' for it was part of the deal."

"I reckon you'll be more careful in the future. Bill's fixin' a place in that stand of blackjack, ten miles or so back. We might as well head that way."

"Fine with me. But, the troops should make it that far by noon. Hell of a time to stop."

"You said, yourself, that a regular blue norther was makin' up. From the looks of this, I think you're right. In that case, they'll be lucky to get that far."

The fury of the storm had increased in the scant few minutes the two men had conversed. Wind whipped the falling flakes into swirling walls of white. Visibility had dropped to under a hundred yards. Overhead, black bellies roiled as they unloaded thicker showers of soft, wet snow. A full-scale blizzard, the scout realized sinkingly. For a moment, he had a disturbing image of the column, caught suddenly in this world of sightless cold. He hoped Dave Roberts would halt them quickly, before any of the green troopers fresh from Jefferson Barracks wandered off.

Chapter 6

Grimly silent, Eli Holten and Tommy Red Hawk stuck to the fastest pace their mounts could safely sustain in the howling maelstrom of the blizzard. With only a vague sense of orientation, the two scouts retraced the scant trail. Their visibility shrank to a hundred feet. Then to fifty. Snow packed on their hats and against the backs of their coats. Their horses' rumps wore white blankets. The big flakes fell thicker. Noon came and they had not yet found Bill Fletcher.

"About another mile, I'd say," Eli told his companion.

"I wonder if we can make that?"

"We have to."

"How do you think the column is doing?"

"I'm afraid to consider it. Davey's smart enough. He'll have 'em pitch tents right where they're stopped."

"It'll be hell without a wind break or wood for a fire."

"Even you couldn't get a fire going in this," Eli retorted.

Tommy swiveled his head from side to side, as though seeing the storm for the first time. "You know something? I think you're right."

"Keep going. We'll lose our sense of direction if we stop too long."

Another fifteen minutes passed and a dark, irregular mass began to loom out of the whirling whiteness. Eli pointed.

"The blackjack. Not far now."

When they neared the trees, Eli saw a faint, flickering tongue of yellow light. Somehow, Bill Fletcher had managed to build a fire. They came closer and, for a moment, the wind dropped to a mild breeze. Through the slanting snowfall, Eli saw the reason for Bill's good fortune.

Fletcher had made a three-sided, roofed-over lean-to from a tarp and two blankets. Fresh-cut pine branches protected it from the worst effects of the blizzard. In its shelter, he had kindled a small fire of twigs and green pine boughs. He sat close to it, wrapped in a large buffalo robe, absorbing the scant warmth. Fletcher looked up at their approach.

"Thought you might have gone to ground," he observed.

"No. Wanted to get back here. When this slackens, I'll try to reach the column."

"What if it don't let off before dark?"

"If that's the case, I'll go anyway by mid-afternoon. They'll need someone to lead them here."

"I don't envy you that job," Fletcher said sincerely.

"I could send you," Eli suggested.

"What? And feel guilty about it for the next month? I know you too well for that, Eli."

Holten flashed a narrow, white slash of smile. "Got any whiskey? I feel like hell."

"You don't look too good, either. There's some white corn in that saddle bag. It'll take the chill off."

"Boy, do I need that," Tommy exclaimed, moving toward the indicated leather pouch.

"*One* swallow, Tommy."

"*Eli!*"

"Only one. My throat's so raw it's become one big sore."

56

"You need some black root," Tommy suggested, referring to the long root of the purple coneflower, used by the Dakota as a general specific against mouth and throat pains.

"I have some in my possibles pouch. I'll mix it with the whiskey."

"Truth of the matter is, Eli, you should stay here an' keep warm. We can close off that other end, leave a smoke flap. Then Tommy an' me can go after the soldier boys."

"It's my job, Bill."

"You look like something an alley cat wouldn't fight over. An' two of us stand a better chance than one."

"You make a good case, Bill. Only I'm over-riding this one. I'll rest here until two-thirty, then head east."

"Hard-headed. That's what you are, Eli. A hard head and a stubborn brain."

"Next thing, you'll be tellin' me my ears are too long and that I bray at the moon."

"*I* didn't say anything about a jackass. But now you mention it . . ."

Missing his bead-decorated, woven willow branch backrest, Spotted Horse leaned back on one arm. He sat, snug and warm, in the small lodge he carried on the war path. Barely five feet tall, a single pony could carry cover, poles and all accessories. Outside, the wind howled and snow flurries blinded a man for any distance beyond the small circle of tipis. He grunted at the oddness of this blizzard and reached for a meaty venison rib.

"It is not yet *Hik 'omini*, yet the snow falls thick," he observed to the two men seated with him.

Bear Heart, stocky and muscular, livened his round face with a greasy smile. He smacked his lips and reached for another hunk of roast meat. Despite the tight lodge cover, the fire flickered fretfully in the blasts of icy wind.

"The *nia'tha* will be shut up tight in their iron road lodges," he mouthed around a big bite of juicy venison. "What difference if it is not the Freezing Moon. This storm works for us."

"He's right," Eats-His-Horse growled. "The whites will not expect anyone to attack them with much snow on the ground. *Heammawihio* favors us with this storm."

"Let's hope so. *Pun u* this early can make for a long winter," Spotted Horse replied. "We must make meat for our lodges."

"First we chase off the *nia'tha*, then we make meat. The Big Freezing Moon is yet far away," Bear Heart advised.

Spotted Horse gave him a warm smile. They had been friends since early childhood. They had swum together, fished and hunted, fought mock battles side-by-side or back-to-back. At thirteen, they had loved the same girl and fought over her, each emerging from the battle with scratches and bloodied noses. Then they had laughed about it and went to wash off in the creek, an arm around each other's shoulder. The girl later became wife to another man and they each married happily. Both had counted coup and killed an enemy in the same battle and entered the Red Shields society.

"I can always trust my good Bear Heart to speak for war. Have the boys keep the ground scraped clear for our ponies. When the storm ends, we will attack the iron road again."

Weakened by his illness, Eli Holten started out into the featureless whiteness of the raging blizzard. Some sixth sense, engendered by twenty years on the prairie, kept his course relatively true. Sonny whuffled and pranced in the knee-deep snow, floundered his way through drifts and rolled his eyes in trepidation. Holten clung to the saddle horn with one hand, the reins wrapped tightly around the other. If he lost his horse, he would die. That he knew only too well. Despite the blinding sameness of land and sky and the fog in his head, he urged his mount forward. He had traveled for a bit over an hour when he heard the faint, muffled sound of human voices.

The column. It had to be. Yet, the wind-whipped words came from off to his right. He had drifted from the regular trail. Eli opened his mouth to yell. Only a pain-bringing croak came out. He heard the jingle of trace chains and more shreds of conversation. Numbed with cold, fearing frostbite, Eli made the tremendous effort of drawing his Remington revolver. Hampered by the glove on his hand, he drew back the hammer and aimed the piece into the air.

Three shots followed each other into the thick wool silence of the storm. Time seemed to creep for him.

"Corp . . . of th . . . guard!" Tatters of words came in the familiar challenge. "Pos . . . ber . . . six!"

He'd made it. Holten cocked his six-gun and fired the remaining two cartridges.

"It came from over this way, Sergeant," a youthful voice sounded from close by several seconds later. Through eyes slitted close against the vicious weather, Eli saw the pale yellow glimmer of a kerosene lantern. He nudged Sonny with his knees and the stout Morgan stallion headed toward the light.

"It's . . . it's Mister Holten," the young soldier declared a moment later.

"Be Ja-zus, he must be near to frozen. Lend a hand there, lad. Lead his horse back to the camp. Captain Roberts will be glad to see him, I'm a-thinkin'."

59

Wrapped in blankets, a cup of hot coffee in his hands, Eli Holten still shivered as he talked with Dave Roberts and Winn Stone. "Fletcher and Red Hawk are holed up some seven miles from here. They have shelter and a fire. How'd you manage this?" Eli gestured with his cup to indicate the subject of his question.

"Bless Sergeant Bigelowe, who didn't think it fit and proper to cook over nothing but an open fire. He brought along a three burner wood stove with the farrier's equipment." Dave Roberts informed him. "After we're finished here, I'm going to put you in the mess tent alongside it to thaw out."

"You made good time. I didn't expect to find you so far along."

"If we hadn't, you'd have been a block of ice long before you got to us. Damn, Eli, that was a dangerous thing to do."

"Had to get back. Too easy for people to get lost in a blizzard."

A frown creased Dave's smooth forehead. "When we finally stopped, a quick muster indicated some fifteen men had wandered off in the snow. No one saw them leave the column. Hell, for a while there no one could see his hand at arm's length. We fired shots and hollered, but none of the missing showed up."

"We'll look for them when the storm's over."

"*We* might. You had better stay close to that stove until you get over what ails you."

"I've got a job to do, same as you, Davey."

"Horse shit. You won't be any good to us dead."

"I'll not argue that point."

"Good. See you don't. Now, down that coffee and I'll have Sergeant Chalmers take you to the mess tent."

Eli's eyelids drooped and the scene blurred before him. His head lolled loosely on his neck and he could hardly form words.

"Tha's good cof-coffee, Davey," he mumbled before he slipped into unconsciousness, his body wracked by fever and the onset of delirium.

Wearing a top hat, morning coat and a wide red silk sash around his waist, Sterling Philliphant grandly escorted his daughter, Gwenivere, to the elegant private car at the end of a short train that waited on the tracks at the Omaha, Nebraska depot. He walked to all appearances as though to the unheard beat of a brass band. Beside him, his lovely daughter smiled sweetly and held the wide brim of her lace-trimmed hat against the frigid gusts of wind that slammed down from the northwest. Somewhere out there, her father had told her, there would be a tremendous snow storm.

"I still object to you coming along, Gwen," Philliphant said in a rich tenor voice. "It's entirely too dangerous."

"Daddy, we've been over this enough. How better to convince the workmen there *is* no danger than to bring your daughter along? Brendon Llewellyn said that the crews were upset over the Indian raids. Some property has been destroyed and a few men injured. So far there've been no deaths. There's no reason I won't be safe."

"*So far* are the operative words, Gwen. Who knows what might happen out there next time? All the same, you know I can never refuse you anything."

"Daddy, I can ride and shoot and run a locomotive. You raised me like a son. Something that for a while I resented. Now, I'm glad for the opportunity. Your surveyors, ballastmen, hoggers, swampers and gandy dancers don't know my background. They'll look at me as I appear to be; a fragile, sweet young thing from

61

back East. They'll want to protect me and, in the process, forget about their own worries."

Sterling Philliphant snorted with cynical laughter. "You're a calculating one, Gwen."

"Only when it comes to helping my Daddy."

"Good morning, Mister Philliphant, Miss Philliphant," the conductor mumbled obsequiously.

"Good morning, Andrew. The boiler making up?"

"Oh, yes, sir. We're ready to pull out soon as you're aboard."

"Fine. Fine. See to it, then." Philliphant gave a hand to his daughter and they boarded the fancy private car.

Inside, dark wood wainscoting and rich flocked wallpaper replaced the usual tongue-in-groove pine and stamped tin decor of a standard passenger car. Crystal chandeliers hung in the parlor section, with plush velvet furniture, ornate side tables and a highly polished pot-belly stove. A sideboard held crystal decanters and glasses. Beyond were a dining room, berths to sleep six people, a commode, cubbyhole kitchen and a pantry. Gwen seated herself on a small settee and arranged the skirt of her high-fashion dress around her.

"Can Regis bring us coffee and some sweet rolls? I swear, Daddy, you took me away from the hotel so fast. I'll starve if we have to wait until dinner time."

"I think we can manage something, Gwen," Philliphant replied as he reached for the bell cord.

A tall, lean, long-faced man with shining ebony skin responded to the summons. "Yassuh?"

"Regis," Philliphant responded, "can we have coffee and something to break our fast served in here, please?"

Regis spread a white grin across his dark face. "Yassuh. I've got bran muffins, sausage pastries an' biscuits, fresh out of the oven."

"Ummm," Gwen delighted. "That sounds good. Bring some of them all. And a pot of butter."

"Right away, Miss."

From the head of the train, the locomotive whistle sounded a shrill command, three shorts and a long.

Far forward from the President's car, in the boxcar provided to transport new workers to the railhead, a motley group of recruits huddled together. They wore a variety of clothing, from faded blue galluses to linsey-woolsey trousers, brogans and flour sack shirts. Few had heavy coats, fewer still any food.

"Do ye have any more of that bread left, Archie?" one heavy County Cork accent inquired of the gangling teenager seated beside him.

"Ouch-na, Uncle Brian, it's hard as a rock and stale as last week's beer."

"Better than an achin' belly," Brian confided. "Would ye look at those three dandies."

Brian O'Dwyer, Archie Boyne's uncle and fresh off the boat like the youth, pointed surreptitiously toward three men somewhat better dressed than the other new employees of the Platte River and Pacific Railroad. The trio huddled with several older, experienced railroad workers, talking quietly.

"Did you hear about the Indian troubles?" the oldest of the three threw out casually.

"What Indian troubles," a bass voice demanded.

"Rumor has it that the Platte River and Pacific has run afoul of the redskins. That we're replacements for men killed or wounded."

"I've not heard that before. Are ya sure, man?"

"No-o. Nothin's sure as of now. We'll see, though, won't we?"

Brian and Archie studied these seeming outsiders.

They wore the remnants of once fine suits of clothes. Here a vest, there a pair of spats. All had good frock coats, though two had frayed cuffs. The speaker wore a bowler hat, while his companions affected low-crown beavers. Their faces were hard, though, with a toughness that belied their being gentry fallen on hard times.

"There's a trio of trouble, I'm a'thinkin'," Brian muttered quietly.

Another peremptory hoot came from the locomotive and the car gave a lurch as the train began to move.

"Sure, Arthur, an' we're put up in all the luxury of the president o' the line himself," the shifty-eyed, thin-lipped member of the trio observed sarcastically.

"Don't be critical, Liam," the one called Arthur answered. "After all, we should be grateful we're not riding on a flatcar."

"It's gonna get cold," Liam responded.

"That it is. But with such plush accommodations, what have we to worry about?"

Their carping banter drew grumbles from the other men, which the increasing clack, rattle and creak of the accelerating train drowned out. Arthur raised his voice to call the attention of those in the car.

"Do you all have your meal chits? We'll be dining on the largess of Mister Philliphant this noon. Don't lose 'em, lads. Oh, and we're off to see the redskins."

Chapter 7

What was it? Warm and bright against his face. Eli Holten opened one eye, which watered instantly, and shut it quickly. Sunlight. By God, real golden sunlight, streaming in through an open tent flap. He groaned.

Captain Dave Roberts came forward, knelt beside his friend. "You're awake. I saw your eye open. No more time to shirk your duty, old pal."

"Go away. I hurt everywhere."

"Lung fever. That's what Doc Lewis says. You won't be up and around for a while, Eli. But you can take some broth, build strength."

"There's a small deerskin pouch in my saddle bags. Bring it here. Also, have Sgt. Bigelow heat me some water."

"You gonna shave?"

"Little Oglala brew for lung fever, or the equivalent of it. That and some stew would be nice."

"Doc said thin broth."

"Fuck that. I want something with strength in it."

"Easy, Eli. The blizzard's ended. Rest and get stronger. Tomorrow, the next day, we'll be able to move on."

"What about the missing men?"

65

"Bill Fletcher and Tommy Red Hawk rode in early this morning. They have men out searching."

"Good. I'll join them this afternoon."

"You will like hell."

"Don't tie my hands. It's my job to get them back."

"Eli, there's a lot more of us than you. Forget it for now."

Holten's eyes narrowed. "You threatening to hold me by force?"

"If I . . . uh, no. Not that way, Eli. It's for your own good, man, and it's the doctor's orders."

The scout started to rise up, only to fall back with a small sigh. "Awh, hell, Davey, I'm weak as a new-born colt. You win this one. But get me my Sioux medicine, eh?"

Eli managed the evil-smelling brew he concocted and a bowl of thick bean soup, with bits of bacon in it. Then he slipped into a fretful sleep that lasted until late into the afternoon. When he awoke for the second time, he began to cough violently. His efforts produced great gobs of phlegm, which he spat into an empty peach can. The mess sergeant sent word of his condition and Dave Roberts arrived soon, along with Lieutenant Stone.

"See? I told you this would . . ." a prodigious cough interrupted. "Be fit as ever by tomorrow. Too bad our own pill rollers won't accept this cure."

"I'll admit you look a hell of a lot better than six hours ago."

"Why, thank you, Davey. Any word on the missing troopers?"

"Not yet. Darkness has called off the search."

"I'll get on it in the morning."

"Only if Doc Lewis says so."

"We'll see about . . . awh, to hell with it." Eli slumped back and closed his eyes. In a moment he

66

slept peacefully, as though not struggling to overcome pneumonia.

Crystal goblets and fine bone china glowed in the soft, yellow light of kerosene lamps. The vibrations generated by the moving train caused the water in the glasses and the soup in shallow bowls to form sets of concentric rings, as though someone had cast a pebble into a pond. Dressed in formal evening clothes, Sterling Philliphant sat across the dining room table from his daughter. He spoke with Augustus Bonner, an investor in the PR&PR, who traveled in the pullman car ahead of the president's private accommodations.

"Yes, there's Indian troubles, damnit. In a way, I can't blame *them* for that. All this," Philliphant waved expansively to indicate the vast prairie beyond the rail car. "All of this was theirs once. We've taken it away."

"That's an odd attitude for a railroad tycoon," Bonner observed in a mildly indignant tone.

"Tycoon? Hell, I was managing director of the Pennsie Line for fifteen years before I decided to start my own rail empire. Huh! Empire indeed. I don't know how to think like a Morgan, or Stanford, or Dodge. Once there were a hundred buffalo for every Indian. Now there's a hundred Indians for every buff. Building the transcontinental railroads played a hell of a lot in changing things around like that. From a humanitarian standpoint, what ever gave us the right to do that?

"Still," Philliphant continued after a thoughtful pause, "there's no stopping westward expansion. And new towns need the most modern facilities. That includes railroads."

"You've a good point there."

"There's more. I figure that if someone has to build

'em, why not someone who is concerned."

"The day Daddy met the bonding requirement with the first hundred miles of track laid, he donated five thousand dollars to Carlsyle."

"Who's Carlsyle?"

"Carlsyle Institute. A school for Indian boys, from first grade to college."

"Well, I'll be damned."

"Maybe you should be," Philliphant snapped, embarrassed by his daughter's revelation. "But that's between you and your Maker. Augie, the reason I asked you to come along is that I want the stockholders to get a first-hand report. I want them to understand that there's better ways of dealing with the Indians than exterminating them."

"You're an idealist," Bonner accused.

"I prefer to consider myself a romantic. Will you do it? Will you keep an open mind while I deal with these raids by the Cheyenne?" Philliphant's intense, hazel eyes glowed as he locked his gaze on the investor.

Portly and balding, Augustus Bonner felt uncomfortable under the burning scrutiny of the PR&PR president. Philliphant's leonine shock of curly gray hair covered an over-large head, with the commanding eyes the principal feature, along with a wide, generous mouth. He must have been a fighter in his earlier days, the stockholder thought. His ideas might work. If only he doesn't turn into a crusader for the redskins. Aware that Philliphant's question had not been rhetorical, Bonner fumbled a tardy reply.

"Um, er, I suppose that's the least I can do. But, we stand to lose a lot of money if extended delays occur. Hundreds of thousands."

"I'm aware of that. I can't indemnify the whole damned works. I don't have that kind of money. This may not, hell it sure won't be the only time we encounter setbacks. But, based on the way I deal with it, what I want is an agreement that we ride out whatever happens in the future and avoid a lot of bloodshed."

"Hummm. I hope you know what you're doing."

"I think I do. Now, let's finish off this soup before it gets cold."

"I don't like it one damn bit," Doctor Lewis grumbled when confronted by Eli Holten early in the morning. The major's insignia on his shoulder boards looked as though they had been frost-covered only moments before.

"You don't have to. All you have to do is approve it," Eli fired back. "Listen. No rattles, no gurgles. My chest is clear, so's my nose. No more sore throat. I've even given up coughing for a while."

"You're still a hell of a long way from well."

"Look, Quint, we all have our job to do. You've done yours. Mine's out there searching. If I lay back here biding my time while those troopers are lost and freezing, Frank Corrington's gonna have my ass."

"You've a point," the doctor agreed reluctantly. "Frank never slacks off on himself in the field. Sometimes to his detriment. All right. You can go. Only, for your sake, stop and take a short rest every hour."

"Thanks, Quint. I knew you'd see it my way."

"By the way, what was that vile-smelling concoction you took yesterday?"

"Oh, a little powdered black root, borage, calamus and sweet flag. You ought to look into their healing properties. I know this Oglala medicine man . . ."

"Get-outta-here!"

"Thanks, Quint."

Outside the tent, Second Lieutenant Gordon

Harris, two months fresh out of the Point, waited with the other two scouts, Corporal Delaney and sixteen troopers. "Search party ready, sir," he rapped out in a high tenor that spoiled the effect.

"You needn't salute me, or sir me, Mister Harris. I'm Eli to everyone who knows me, *Mister* Holten to those who don't. I believe your first name's Gordon?"

"Yes, sir, uh, that's right, Eli."

"Good. Quick on the up-take. We'll get along, Gordon. How do you propose to conduct the sweep?"

"I thought we'd divide up, take half out in a circular pattern, along each side of our back trail."

"Humm. Fair enough. Bill, Tommy, go with Delaney and eight troopers. Take the south side of the trail. Use a zig-zag pattern, instead of a spiral. We'll do likewise on the north."

"Why not a spiral search, uh, Eli?"

"Too easy to pass by someone. They aren't exactly going to be standing up hollerin' for help. If they're still alive, chances are they'll be huddled up somewhere tryin' to keep warm."

"Right! I never thought of that."

"You've never searched for men lost in a blizzard before, I'll wager. Let's move 'em out, Lieutenant."

Muted, made fuzzy and indistinct by the thick blanket of white, the prairie had lost all its prominent features. Harsh sunlight reflected off the snowy mantle, punishing the eyes of the searchers, and making their task more difficult. The harsh climate had given no quarter. The horses, belly deep in snow, plowed through drifts with difficulty. They snorted in protest, white plumes streaming from their flared nostrils. Half an hour out from camp, Eli Holten found the first victim.

Curled in a ball, a thin blanket pulled over him, the soldier lay frozen to death. Although his features had darkened, he looked at peace.

"My God," Gordon Harris gasped. "It's . . . it's awful."

"Get used to it, Gordon. We'll probably find a lot more like him. Evans, wasn't it? Company D?"

"Yeah. I think so. Do we send him back now?"

"I suppose we should. Take only one man."

"He looks so . . . undisturbed by it all," the green young officer said in a near-whisper.

"They say it's a peaceful way to go. Only how do *they* know, unless they're already beyond communicating with us?"

"Over here," a trooper called from a hundred yards away.

"Another one," Eli acknowledged regretfully.

Once the two corpses had been arranged on a spare horse, a trooper was detailed to take them back to camp. Eli and the remainder rode on. Twenty minutes passed without locating any more bodies. Muffled shots sounded in the distance, from the opposite side of the trail.

"Delaney's found someone," Eli suggested.

"Or some trooper in his detail got lost," Harris countered.

"You're learning," Eli quipped with a grin.

Ponderously, through the drifts and hidden drop-offs, the grim task went on. Three men appeared suddenly, from a deep wash, shouting and waving blankets over their heads. They showed no embarrassment when tears of relief and joy ran down their faces. Neither did Lieutenant Harris. Even Eli Holten had his vision blurred by moisture that rose, but didn't spill over. He cleared his throat roughly to jog free a sudden tightness.

"Did you men manage to protect your horses?"

"Sure did. They're down in the draw. We're hungry

71

enough to have eaten one of them. But they're just as bad off," a corporal responded.

"Jenkins, isn't it? C Company?"

"Right, Mister Holten."

"Camp's about five miles due west of here. Get organized and head that way. There'll be hot food and plenty of *Ariosa* waiting."

A mile further on, a white-covered spectre rose from the ground and limped toward the searchers. Holten fought off the chill that had penetrated his heavy coat and urged Sonny forward. He reached the lucky soldier in scant moments.

"Funny, I can't feel my feet any more. But my nose is on fire."

The scout studied him closely. Frostbite. Brighter red than any town drunk's, the soldier's nose had split along one side and oozed a thin ribbon of blood and fluid, frozen in a static trickle by the icy wind. He probably wouldn't lose it, but it would never again win a beauty prize. What about the feet? Holten dismounted and motioned for the trooper to sit on his blanket.

"Let's get a look at your toes."

"Uh . . . you don't think . . . ?"

"Off with the boots, soldier."

"Yes, sir, Mister Holten."

Both feet had the same cherry hue of the man's nose. He'd been lucky that far. Three toes, though, had become blackened and gnarled. Frostbitten to death. They'd have to come off, Eli realized, or the man would never make it through the day. Two on one foot, one on the other. It bought the man an instant return to civilian life. Eli knelt to examine the injuries closer.

"Soldier, I've got some bad news for you. You're going to be a civilian by morning."

"Uh . . . then . . . it's what I figgered, eh?"

72

"Frostbite. Yep. Three toes. And they're going to have to come off now." Holten rose and shouted to the search party. "Lieutenant Harris, over this way!"

When the young officer arrived, Eli explained the situation briefly. "It's the only way, Gordon. I'll have to do it with my Bowie."

"Good God, man. How can he survive that?"

"No better or worse than if Doc did it with a scalpel. Do you have any whiskey along?"

Harris flushed, his response flustered. "That's against regulations, Eli. You know that."

"Sure I do. And I'll ask again. Do you have any whiskey along?"

"Uh . . . well, uh, Doc Lewis suggested I bring some brandy along. For medicinal purposes, you understand."

"Right. Hand it over."

Eli took the flask, along with his canteen and pouch of Sioux medical herbs. He gave the liquor to the afflicted soldier and told him to drain it all. Then he mixed a thick paste of wormwood, calamus and dock weed root, which he smeared on the damaged toes and well up each foot. It would assure numbness when the time came.

"How's it going with the brandy, trooper?"

"Pretty good, Mis'er Holten, Hits hard on an emp'y stomach."

"Need any help with it, let me know."

"What d'you n-need it for?"

"Hell, I'm the one's got to take these toes off."

"Jesus."

"Another big gulp, right?"

"Ri-ight."

Eli drew his Bowie in a smooth move, raised one leg and swiftly cut through flesh and the second joint of the victim's right little toe. Another flick of the blade and

73

the one next to it fell into the snow. Holten clamped a calamus-saturated wad of gauze to the bleeding stumps and fastened that in place with strips of rawhide.

"That'll hold until we get him back to Doc Lewis. Now the other one. Drink up."

The scout turned to see that his patient had passed out. He picked up the brandy flask and took a long swallow. A swipe with the back of his hand cleaned his face and he bent to the other leg. It took less time and he soon had the unconscious man bandaged.

"Get him back fast," Eli told Harris. "God, how I hate doing something like that. I'd never make a doctor."

"Regular sawbones," Harris gritted. He wanted to throw up. "You gonna save the toes?"

"What for?"

"Burial, of course."

"Haven't time. Unless you want to carry them around all day."

"Uh . . . no. Forget it."

"Let's keep going. We've more work to do."

Chapter 8

Hat in hand, Andrew McMahon, the conductor stood in the front doorway to Philliphant's private car. The president of the railway held an expression that looked like his employee had said something extremely nasty.

"*Snow*, did you say?"

"Yes, Mister Philliphant. Charlie, the engineer, said it was almost a sure thing we'd run into some snow ahead. That was about an hour ago. Then Howard in the express car snagged this message at the last depot." He handed a folded slip of paper to Philliphant.

The president of the PR&PR unfolded it and read.

HEAVY SNOWS WEST OF A LINE THROUGH BUTTE NEBRASKA AND THROUGHOUT DAKOTA TERRITORY X ADVISE CAUTION PERHAPS HOLD OVER A DAY IN GREGORY D T XX JENNINGS

"All we need is a little more delay," Philliphant grumbled at the advisory from his traffic manager.

What the devil would Jennings know about it in Omaha? Only what the telegraph sent. He could definitely not afford to be late. Wait, hadn't they already passed Butte? They should be in the territory by now.

"Andrew, haven't we passed through Butte?"

"Yes, sir. That's where Howard got this message from."

"Do you see any snow?"

"Uh . . . no sir. Nothing but bare ground. It's sure cold though."

"That's another matter entirely. I'll wager the snow fell far west of us. How far to Gregory?"

"An hour or so, Mister Philliphant. A little over twenty miles."

"We're not moving at all fast," the president complained.

"We've a load of rail up front, Mister Philliphant. Charlie's got the throttle wide open."

"Oh, fine. Just fine. Snow that isn't there and a laggard train. Does wonders for the fire in my stomach."

"An ulcer, sir?"

"Harumph! Not so's I'd notice, Andrew. You let me know if you encounter any snow, eh?"

"Oh, yes, sir," the conductor replied, unaware that his employer had been facetious.

The remainder of the day crawled along in like pace. Bright lamps in the private car and smaller ones in the public coaches made moving rectangles of yellow on the ground after the sun had lowered in the west. At least by morning, Sterling Philliphant consoled himself, they would be another two hundred miles toward their goal. Snow, indeed. In October?

"What would happen if we did run into snow, Daddy?" Gwen inquired at the supper table.

"Stop us cold. At least any large drifts would. Sounds to me like some bored spark driver got a wild hair and decided to shake up everyone down the line. I'm having Bonner and some gentlemen in for whist after we dine, my dear. Will you be hostess and do the honor of being my partner?"

"Yes, Daddy. I'd be glad to."

"Snow. Ridiculous."

Sunrise two hundred miles further down the track revealed the identical monotonous sameness of the rolling prairie as seen the previous sundown. The graded and ballasted right-of-way for the PR&PR created an ugly, raw slash through the waving brown grass. Here and there small patches of white flashed highlights.

"Snow," Gwen Philliphant declared triumphantly.

"But not in the quantity we were warned about," her father countered.

Something else impinged on their morning coffee.

"Look, Daddy, Indians," Gwen declared, pointing off at an oblique angle from the front of the train. "They're riding toward the tracks."

"Want to get a look at the iron horse, I suppose."

"They, uh, don't look entirely friendly."

Sterling Philliphant leaned closer to the window. "Hummm. I don't think they're Sioux. What is this anyway?"

At the head of the stretched out file of warriors, a tall, muscular man released the reins of his pony and brought a tack-studded rifle to his shoulder. Smoke billowed from the muzzle and the crack of detonation could be heard faintly over the rattle of the train.

"By God, he's shooting at us!" Philliphant exploded.

A moment later the door burst open and the conductor ran along the narrow aisle to the livingroom. "Indians, Mister Philliphant. They're attacking the train."

"I can see that, Andrew. Has anyone fired back at them?"

"No, sir."

"Good. See that they don't."

"*Father*, they're shooting at us."

"I know. But we can easily outrun them. Damnit, where's the Army when we need them?"

"You instructed that they meet us at end-of-track, Daddy."

"Then I did a fool thing. They could be rounding up these hostiles and herding them away. How can one operate on a schedule with these nuisance raids going on?"

Like a spurt of hail, three arrows struck the side of the box car.

"Saints above!" a wiry, bow-legged gandy dancer exclaimed. "What's happenin' out there?"

Arthur Lavin replied in a bored tone. "I believe we are being attacked by Indians. Nasty brutes at that. They're shooting arrows at the train. A couple of them have rifles."

"Sure an' I don't like the sound of that."

"Nor I," Liam Daley added in. "I'm beginnin' to wonder if it's wise to be workin' fer this grand Platte River and Pacific. Indian troubles have been known to get a few people killed."

"An' that's a fact," Devon Flynn added. "I didn't sign on to be an Injun fighter."

"Nor I," one of the huddled workmen agreed.

"One thing's for sure," a calm voice injected, "we can outrun them. Horses tire out, locomotives don't."

"So long as we have enough wood aboard," Lavin added grimly.

Charlie Wellman, the engineer, leaned out the right hand cab window and looked back along the train. His lips puckered into an unheard whistle. The damned heathens had scarred his beautiful charge. Inwardly he ached with the desire to plunk a few .44-40 rounds into those redskins.

"Would you look at that. Those redsticks have gone and sunk arrows into my pretty girl. Damn them," he growled aloud, over the roar of the open boiler and the half a dozen other familiar noises of the locomotive.

His fireman looked up from passing wood into the cherry maw of the boiler. "Be glad they didn't put a few in you, Charlie."

Wellman eased open the sanding valve a slight notch to allow a trickle to spill onto the tracks. Right now he could use a little more traction. The Baldwin 4-4-0, No. 4 surged in all its drivers, little puffer-bellies of steam escaping from the big pistons with each stroke. He gave a little nudge to the nickel-plated handle of the throttle and sensed, rather than felt, the increase in speed. The *General Stande Wattie* edged over thirty miles an hour and another glance to the rear assured Charlie that the copper-skinned figures on their galloping horses had begun to shrink to smallness behind the speeding train. Good goin', General, he thought.

That brought a smile to Charlie's face. Ol' Philliphant might be Main Line Philadelphia, but he had chosen for some reason to christen his locomotives after *Confederate* generals. He had the *General Lee*, *T. J. Jackson*, *JEB Stewart*, and *Stande Wattie*. Quite a collection. The latter had been named for the last Confederate general to surrender at the end of the war. Charlie frowned over his reflections. Stande Wattie had been a Cherokee. An Indian. And Indians had just attacked them. There was no justice in the world.

Weakened by his ordeal, Eli Holten barely managed to remain in the saddle during the rest of the search for the missing men. When he awakened that morning, he had ached all over, as though never being aboard a horse before. A slight cough had returned. He also experienced a burning sensation deep in his chest. Innate caution kept him from mentioning these symptoms to Major Lewis. The doctor, Eli felt, had enough to deal with. The detail worked for two hours and located nothing but three corpses.

Truth to tell, Eli believed, that's all they would find. Too much time had gone by. His cough grew worse and he began to slip into dizziness. By mid-morning, he swayed drunkenly in the saddle. Lieutenant Harris cantered over to him, a worry frown furrowing the young officer's brow.

"You look like hell, Eli."

"Feel like it, too, Gordon. Good thing the sun's melting this snow."

"Nice to see the ground again," Harris agreed.

Three shots sounded in rapid succession from beyond a low swale. Harris jerked his head that direction. Eli moved more slowly, regretting the necessity. Whirling landscape made his stomach lurch. Gaining tenuous control over his ailing body, he tapped Sonny with his spurs and set out to investigate.

"Get some men up here," Eli croaked hoarsely when he topped the rise. "There's four of 'em. A couple look rather bad off."

Harris rode up beside him. "More dead than alive." He turned and signaled to some of the search party.

"We wandered around in circles for two days," one survivor forced out as he climbed laboriously toward them. "Must a walked twenty miles. Then the melt

80

today let us get our bearings. Headed the right way after that."

"Where are your horses?" Lt. Harris demanded.

"Dead or run off, Lieutenant. Uh, sir, there's two boys down there that's hurt purty bad. Don't know if one'll make it at all."

Harris glanced over at Eli, who blinked his eyes owlishly, his features slack. "You're not much better. I'm sending you back with these four and the two we picked up by the creek."

"I'll manage."

"No, you won't. That's the problem, Eli. I'll get Bill Fletcher over here to scout for me. You and these men have to get back to camp."

"Uh . . . I'd argue that with you, Gordon, but right now I . . ." Eli let the sentence hang unfinished, as though he had forgotten what he wanted to say.

"That's one argument you just lost," Harris said firmly.

Horses were brought up for the surviving soldiers and they helped the weaker ones to mount. With Eli Holten in the lead, the small file started out to the trail and westward to the camp. The search had taken them ten miles from the bivouac and at a walking pace, time worked its ravages on the scout.

By the time the tents were in sight, Eli had slumped forward on his horse's neck, coughing incessantly, eyes bright with fever, his cheeks flushed. Concern among the soldiers for their sick companions shifted to him. Doctor Lewis swore mighty, colorful oaths when he saw Eli's condition.

"He's a pluperfect idiot! Damn his stubbornness. Whatever the hell that was you took, Eli, it only treated the symptoms, not the disease. I'm a fool for letting you go out these last two days."

"Gotta . . . gimme . . . some more," Eli mumbled.

His chest heaved with the effort of his breathing.

"I'll give you laudanum and keep you asleep 'till you heal, you rock-headed numbskull."

"Jis' gimme my pouch. Gotta . . . clear my . . . lungs."

Growling, the doctor complied, adding to the potion a large dollop of laudanum. The opiate acted swiftly on Holten's weakened constitution. Doc Lewis grunted in satisfaction as the scout slipped off to sleep. Then he directed men to wrap Eli in blankets and keep him close to the cook tent stove. He would live or die now, as his Maker decreed.

Chapter 9

Four shorts and a long. Three times. Trouble ahead, Sterling Philliphant thought automatically as he heard the locomotive whistle far ahead on the tracks. What now? More Indians?

"I think we've found that heavy snow we were warned about, Daddy," Gwen said lightly as she stepped into the private car. "Big high drifts that are just starting to melt."

"What next? Even nature's out to ruin me."

"Oh, you old sour-puss, it's not *you* that's been singled out. I sure would hate to have been caught out in that when it was coming down, any way but in this car. It's so cold. Not like back home."

"Not to mention freakish. It's only mid-October. Shouldn't have happened at all. I suppose it stopped progress at rail's end. More worries."

Philliphant ceased talking as the train began to slow. He shook his head in impatience. What could Charlie be up to?

Andrew McMahon knocked and entered. "Big drift ahead, Mister Philliphant. We're gonna have to off-load the new workmen and put 'em at it with shovels."

"Can't Charlie blast through with the cow-catcher?"

"No, sir. Snow in a cutbank higher than the smoke-stack."

"If we had dual tracks and a snowplow, delays like this wouldn't happen," the president said thoughtfully. "Well, get on with it. We're running late as it is."

"Yes, sir."

Raw, yellow subsoil lay bare to the sky where the railroad crews had blasted and dug the way through a low rise to maintain the grade level. The blizzard had nearly filled the notch with drifted snow. Andrew McMahon went forward and rolled open the boxcar door.

"All right, fellers, you start earnin' your pay as of now. Everybody out. Grab a shovel and start digging that snow out of the way."

Loud grumbles, a railroader's prerogative, answered him. Nevertheless, accustomed to such exigencies, the men complied. Three of them, Andrew noticed, held back a bit. Better dressed than the others, they seemed to have a furtive air to Andrew's experienced eye. Like yard rats or the tramps who rode the rods rather than paying customers. He hadn't liked them much when they signed on in Omaha. Their unwillingness to share in the other men's toils did nothing to improve his opinion. Under his direct scrutiny, they reluctantly lined up to receive shovels.

"Me? Digging out snow?" Arthur Lavin muttered quietly. "I haven't worked with my hands in years. It's an imposition. An indignity."

"Fancy him," Devon Flynn riposted. " 'Haven't worked with my hands in years.' Sure an' how did you expect to manage at the railhead without a bit of work with yer hands?"

"You do your part, I'll do mine. That's why I'm the boss and you're only a strong arm."

"Don't be gettin' uppity, now. I was lookin' for a job when I took this one. I can look again."

"With two broken legs?"

84

"Ouch, now. And it would be meself havin' to go about the breakin'. That's what you labor johnnies—oops! shouldn't say that—hired me for ain't it?"

"Flynn, you run your mouth too much. Some of these roustabouts hear you use that word and the game's up. Now take a shovel and let's make like we're doin' our share."

Wet, thick and heavily compacted, the snow moved like water-soaked cotton. Progress could be measured in inches. As the men toiled, the snow higher up would break off and tumble down. For every foot forward, they lost six inches. The workmen began to sweat from their labor, while their breath made frosty smoke in the air. To take off their heavy coats was to invite pneumonia. Muscles not used in a long while began to protest. Liam Daley was first to complain.

"Saints above, a fireman's not got it so hard, even in a locomotive race. Me back feels like it's been set on fire. Way we're goin' we could be here until the middle of tomorrow."

"You can't be talkin' and workin' at the same time," Andrew McMahon called out. "Get to shovelin'."

"Me back is near unto breakin', Mister Conductor, sir. Sure an' haven't ye ever heard of givin' men a rest? Or work us in relays, half restin' while the other half works?"

"You've a lot of snow to move. No more backtalk, ya hear?"

"Foine way to run a railroad, I say. You could work a man to death at this pace."

"Grumblers and shirkers don't have work on the Platte River and Pacific for long," Andrew warned darkly.

"Speakin' as for right now, I don't see how that is such a bad thing."

"It's a hell of a long walk back to civilization,"

Andrew said simply.

"Ah-ha! Now we've reached the heart of it, eh? It's work or walk? Well, fer meself . . . fer the time bein' at least, I'll take the work."

"You have more of a mouth problem than Devon," Arthur complained.

"Ah, but I did get the thought of unfairness planted in the wee brains of our fellow laborers, did I not?"

"Hummm. You've a point. For a while, keep quiet and make handy with that shovel."

"The snow's melting fast," Eli Holten observed when he came out of his laudanum-induced sleep. "We ought to be moving on. With all this runoff, the trail will be a quagmire. Best bet is to cut due south to the tracks and follow them to the rail head."

"You're still in no shape to travel. Neither are at least seven of the men you rescued," Doc Lewis told the scout.

"When?"

"Another day, two perhaps. You got rid of a lot of liquid, but there's more rattling around inside you. I'd like to be able to take your lungs out and run them through a clothes vise. That's the only quick way to clear you up."

"Much more melt water and those wagons'll sink to the hubs. We should be moving now."

"That one who came in with you, Eli," the doctor went on, ignoring the urgency in Eli's voice. "He's closer to dead than alive. Without a couple of days to improve in, we'd lose him. It's not just you any more."

"I appreciate that, Doc. But, damnit." A seizure of coughing interrupted Holten's protest. When he recovered and wiped his eyes, he went on, panting slightly. "All of us can rest at the railhead. A day, day and a half at most to get there."

"I'll check on my other patients, Eli. That's the most I can offer. If they show improvement, I'll reconsider."

"And you call me stubborn."

Gwen felt like a child again. She had dressed warmly and left the train to examine the snow. Before she had taken a dozen steps away from the track, Gwen found herself compelled to bend down and scoop up the heavy, damp flakes. She compressed a handful into a ball and threw it against the side of the train. Quickly she made another and repeated her act of sacrilege. Then she tittered in merriment and spoke aloud.

"Daddy would be furious over such disrespect."

"Would he now?"

The voice came from behind her. Gwen turned suddenly to confront a man of medium height, slender and better dressed than most workmen. Could he be one of the group with Augustus Bonner? His gray eyes twinkled with shared mischief.

"I wouldn't mind doing that myself," he concluded. "Pardon me. Let me introduce myself. My name is Arthur Lavin." He pronounced his name *La-vine*.

"I'm Gwen Philliphant."

"Ah! The president's daughter. Well, Miss Philliphant, I've recently become an employee of your father's line. Tally clerk if you're familiar with the term."

"You're the one who keeps record of how much track is laid each day? Inventories the number of spikes, bolts and fishplates?"

"Remarkable. That's exactly correct." Lavin removed a bowler hat to run long, ink-stained fingers through his soft brown hair. "You've acquired considerable technical knowledge for a young woman who should have far more pleasant matters to occupy her time."

"Daddy wanted me to have a complete education on what makes a railroad. On this trip, at least, I'm to be his assistant, rather than a passenger."

"I see. Well then, I suppose we'll have occasion to confer often, once I begin my duties. A pleasure speaking with you, Miss Philliphant. Now I must get back to the dreary task of removing that snowbank."

Faint cries of alarm came from the front of the train and the steam whistle hooted the emergency signal. Gwen brought a gloved hand to her mouth and her eyes widened with worry.

"What's happened?"

"I don't know. Something unfortunate, I'm sure. Excuse me." Lavin took off at a trot toward the center of excited activity.

Curious, Gwen followed. Men shouted and flailed at the snow face. A cloud of crystals hung in the air. As she neared, she made out individual voices, calling out the nature of the emergency.

"Cave in," one burly workman declared.

"Whole damn slope broke loose and fell. Caught at least two men under it."

"Who are they?"

"Don't know yet."

"Oh, my!" Gwen exclaimed involuntarily. "They'll suffocate."

Patrick McCrae, the new gang foreman, looked up, surprised by the sound of a woman's voice. "I reckon they will, Miss. If we don't dig them out in time."

"These men look cold and hungry. How can they work fast enough in that condition?"

"Hungry or not, cold or not, they're gonna have to be quick about it if they want to save their comrades' lives."

"Why is it that they have to be like this?"

"Miss? Uh . . . I see. They ride in that boxcar. We all do. No way to fix hot meals or keep too much warm."

"That's awful. Disgraceful. I'll see that something is done about it at once."

McCrae started to chuckle patronizingly, then recognition came. "Uh, Miss, you're Mister Philliphant's daughter, aren't you?"

"That's correct. I'm going to have Regis, that's my father's cook, prepare coffee, soup and sandwiches for these men immediately. And . . ." Gwen went on, planning as she spoke, "and between the pullman car and ours, there's dozens of spare blankets. I'll see they are warmed and sent along, too."

"Why . . . why, that's mighty considerate of you, Miss. But, won't that create some, ah, difficulty?"

"I see no reason why it should." Gwen spotted the conductor and hailed him. When he arrived she quickly outlined her intentions and concluded firmly, "Consider that a direct order, Andrew. Send the brakemen, and other train crew not needed on the snow digging, back to get these things when they're ready."

"Uh, these are your father's orders, Miss Philliphant?"

"They are mine, which is to say the same thing. See to it at once."

"Yes, Miss."

Patrick McCrae grinned broadly and removed his hat in a gesture of respect. "You're a marvel, Miss. Uh, if you'll pardon my sayin' it."

"It's quite all right. I can't abide injustice."

Twenty minutes later, the food began to arrive. Although chilled through and through, Gwen remained at the front of the locomotive, watching intently. Scoops of snow flew in every direction and the men relieved in pairs to eat and refresh themselves never failed to stop by her and make some mumbled offering of gratitude. Her impulsive gesture had won their hearts like nothing else could have. Gwen didn't hear her father's approach.

"Quite a noble gesture, my dear."

Gwen started, then turned to face her parent. "Oh, I didn't know you were here, Daddy."

"I wondered why you had been gone so long. Then when Regis began rattling pots in the kitchen, I inquired into the reason. He told me Andrew had come with orders from you. Naturally I wanted to see the results."

"And?"

"I must say I have been remiss. I never considered the hardship this storm would have on our new workmen. Ordinarily, they get meals at water stops and such. Out here there are none. And the unexpected weather makes their situation worse. Thank you for acting so wisely in my stead."

"You're terribly formal, Daddy."

"I'm terribly embarrassed, Gwen."

Gwen threw her arms around her father's neck and hugged him. "Don't be, Daddy. No harm was done."

A shout came from the center of activity. Coughing and staggering, a teenaged lad, coated in snow, stumbled out from the midst of the workers.

"We got one of them!" Patrick McCrae yelled. A ragged cheer followed.

"Wrap him in one of those blankets and pour some soup down him fast," Arthur Lavin advised.

While Archie Boyne sputtered and shivered, the crew went back to digging. A warning creaking came from the snow above and they jumped back.

"Some of you men get up on the sides and relieve that load, or we'll be back where we started," McCrae ordered.

Bit by bit the heavy drift dwindled. Another lusty bellow announced the discovery of a shoe. One with a foot in it. Within seconds, a spluttering, gagging Devon Flynn emerged from his white grave. Wall-eyed and panting, he staggered toward where Arthur Lavin stood, a steaming bowl of soup in one hand and a blanket in the other.

"All well that ends . . . eh, Gwen," her father remarked. "Another half hour and we should be through that drift. Then full speed ahead."

"I'll be glad when we reach the railhead, Daddy."

"So will we all, my dear."

Chapter 10

Morning exploded over the prairie, bright and warmer. The remaining snow began to melt rapidly. The temperature rose steadily. By noontime, Capt. Dave Roberts began to predict a period of Indian Summer. With the improved climate, the men suffering from exposure started to rally quickly. Doctor Lewis ceased administering laudanum to Eli Holten and the scout returned to conscious control shortly after one in the afternoon.

"I feel like a new man," he declared when the doctor and Captain Roberts visited him.

"More like a new-born pup," the portly medico growled. "Your lungs are still congested, Eli. A few more days rest and everyone will be fit."

"We don't have a 'few more days,' Doc. We have to get to the railhead. The Cheyenne will be quick to take advantage of this change in the weather. This is one time when tactical considerations have to take precedent over medical opinion."

Dave Roberts looked uncomfortable. "I have to agree with Eli this time," he began. "We lost too much time with the storm and searching for strays. The Cheyenne won't be similarly incapacitated. We'll break camp today, move out first thing in the morning."

"Need I remind you that I outrank you, young

man?" Doctor Lewis' tone was icy.

"But you're not in the chain of command, Doc," Eli Holten inserted. "If you strongly disagree with Davey and I, you can write your report and submit it to General Corrington when we return to Fort Rawlins. Otherwise, Davey is in charge."

"All I need is a *civilian* scout and a guardhouse lawyer rolled into one," the doctor grumped. He stumped away, entirely unhappy with what had occurred, though equally aware any such report critical of Eli Holten would fall on unfertile soil if delivered to Frank Corrington.

"Aaagh!" Spotted Horse exclaimed as he finished the last sip of the tea he had made from the *wi iv tsis' to to*. Since the storm had come and they had ridden east to attack the train, he had been troubled by a lingering cough and tickling in his throat. The bitter bite of the juniper remained after he had swallowed. Despite this minor affliction, he felt good.

Only that morning ten members of the *Hotamitaniu* society—the Dog Soldiers—had ridden to join his fight. They came talking of taking scalps. Now he would have to reason with them.

"Kill one *nia'tha* and ten more come to replace him," he began. "If we scare them off, we have won. If we kill them all, we will eventually lose."

"Some men would be told they talk like women if they said that," the leader of the Dog Soldiers taunted dryly. "All *Tsistsistas* know of the bravery of Spotted Horse. *He* would not shun war with the whites. *He* would not withhold his hand from striking a *nia'tha* enemy. Where is there any honor in scaring them?"

"There is much honor in saving our land from the iron road, *Mohkstamoahts*," Spotted Horse answered

93

mildly. He nodded toward the stout, muscular Dog Soldier to Black Bear's right. "Didn't *Mist'aimahan'* win great acclaim when he chased away the seekers of yellow metal?"

Black Bear grunted and rolled his powerful shoulders. "Owl Friend counted coup on three of the *nia'tha*. He shot arrows into five of them."

"Black Bear, we shoot the whites at the iron road. With arrows and bullets. We bend the iron bands, burn the square logs. We've attacked one of their iron horses, while it moved. Soon we'll knock one over on its side. *Things* mean more to the *nia'tha* than people. Before long the whites will grow tired of having their things destroyed. They will give up and leave."

Mohkstamoahts scowled, eyes slitted in deep thought. "I'm not so sure. It is true what you say. For every *nia'tha* who falls, many come to take his place. What does that matter to us? A warrior's way is to fight."

"But not necessarily to die."

"Any day is a good day to die."

"You speak harshly." Spotted Horse bent forward and lifted the ornately carved, colorfully decorated sacred war pipe. "I took up the sacred pipe to fight the whites. Do you come to touch it and fight it at my side? Or did you come to spend our days in argument?"

Black Bear allowed a tiny slit of a smile. "I touch the pipe gladly. To ride at the side of Spotted Horse is a great honor. When do we strike again?"

"Soon, *Mohkstamoahts*. There is a place where the iron horses circle, so that the smoking, hissing head chases the tail. There they turn around to go back to *Ish' i tsisiss' i miis'*. It is at this place we will knock one of them off the iron bands."

Black Bear looked happier. "That iron horse will not go to where the sun comes up. We will smash it and burn everything."

"And the whites will be glad to leave us alone," Spotted Horse concluded.

Black smoke belched from the stack of the *General Stande Wattie*. The polished walking beams of the drivers flashed in the sun as the huge wheels spun in perfect coordination, pulling the train along the track. In the distance, about a mile away, could be seen the dark shapes of the permanent work train. Charlie shrilled a friendly greeting on the steam whistle and urged another notch out of the throttle.

An answering hail welcomed the new arrival. Warm sunlight had caused the workmen to open the doors of the boxcar and two men chanced a cinder in an eye to look along the right-of-way toward their destination.

"It's a right big camp, Uncle Brian," young Archie exclaimed.

"Ye'll not be seein' much more if ye catch a clinker in the eye, Arch. Pull yer head in like a good lad."

Much to Brian's relief, Archie had bounced back from his temporary burial in snow with all the energy of youth. Only in his sleep did he sometimes whimper and make small, clawing gestures, as though attempting to dig his way out. When they had left New York, in the midst of an employment slump, Brian's brother-in-law, Seamus Boyne, had made the boy's safety and conduct a special charge for Brian. Not that he begrudged the responsibility. He loved the lad and wanted only good for him. A bit young, at fourteen, to be a railroader, Brian thought. All the same, many a youth his age had been out and at work full time before they saw their twelfth year. With the good job Seamus had acquired upon arriving from Ireland, and the bit of money Margaret Mary had saved before her marriage, Archie had been lucky.

At least until the localized financial crisis came that laid off two thousand in New York City alone. Throughout New England, tens of thousands were out of work. The effects had not yet spread beyond Pennsylvania, praise be. Yet, moving on to the West seemed the only sensible thing to do. Besides, a stint of hard work, the clean, fresh air of the frontier, would do wonders for the boy.

Archie, a native of Dublin, had a city-dweller's pallor. His muscles had not developed to their fullest playing stick ball or climbing stairs to a third floor flat. He'd fill out, take on weight and have a clear eye when he returned at the end of the next summer. Even the wharf-rat toughs who hung out near the Boyne home in the Bronx would stay clear of Archie after that.

"Uncle Brian, is it true it snows higher than our brownstone out here?"

"Ah, so I've heard, lad. Tis not like Ireland. We be like pilgrims out here, Archie. Best thing to do is keep quiet and listen. Ye learn a lot more that way. And you don't look simple to those what's yer betters."

"If it does, how can we work?" Archie persisted, going back to the subject of snow.

"We won't. At least not out here. Another month and a half and it's back to Omaha. Accordin' to me friend, Patrick McCrae, there'll be track maintenance jobs for us in the yards there. Come the spring thaw and we head back out here. At five miles of track a day, a hundred days will see us past the Rocky Mountains to the point where the Platte River and Pacific ties in with the Denver and Rio Grande, somewhere near the Yellowstone country. That's when we part company with 'em, Archie."

"You've sure learned a lot in a short time, Uncle Brian. But, why do we have to quit then?"

" 'Cause that's all the time I could get yer folks to

agree to let ye be gone. There is a matter of schoolin' ye know."

"Awh, hell, who wants school?"

"You do, if ye don't want to grow up a worthless bum, like yer uncle."

"You're not a bum, Uncle Brian. You're not worthless, either."

"Sure an' I'm glad to hear that from someone. Would ye be kind enough to be tellin' that to Officers Clancy and Doolin the next time you see 'em?"

"It's not your fault you were out of work. Those two are just jealous because you've been a seaman on a merchant ship, a railroader and worked with the circus on the Continent. They were born in this country an' never traveled. Stay-at-homes and too embarrassed to admit it."

Brian puckered his lips and produced a thin whistle. "Got it all figgered out, do ye? Well, an', I suppose ye've got the right of it. All the same, Clancy and Doolin run me in fer vagrancy. His Worship told me to get a job or go to jail. Hadn't been far yer Poppa, I'd been lookin' at the world through iron bars no matter what. Sheer luck to run into Patrick an' learn about this fine line hirin' on."

Archie started to answer, his mind filled with the memory of being buried under all that snow, when the train gave a lurch and began to lose speed. "We're there," the boy cried and rushed to one of the open doors.

Slowly, the *General Stande Wattie* crawled up behind the permanent train. Brakes screeched and steam gushed out in dragon-like hisses. The cars bumped together, elongated and slammed back once more, then stopped. Immediately men began to jump off, arms encumbered with their belongings.

"After they get those rails off the flatcars and stack

97

the ties, I'll take the *General* down the track and through the 'Y', then back in here." Charlie told the conductor. "That way, when we're ready to make the bob-tail run back to Omaha, there won't be any delay."

"Just what Mister Philliphant expected," Andrew told the engineer. "We'll be runnin' with only the locomotive, tender and three flatcars. We ought to make good time goin' to the roundhouse."

"First class, all the way," Charlie assured him.

"Mister Philliphant wants to see the chief construction engineer. If you run into him, send him along."

"Sure will." Charlie consulted his big Ingraham railroader's watch. "This time of day, you'll probably find him in his digs, havin' dinner."

"Never thought of that. No wonder there ain't so many roustabouts swarmin' around. All busy fillin' their faces. I could go for some of that, myself."

"Me, too. Better get our passengers fed, while we're at it."

"Yep. Hey, McCrae. Take the new men up to the cookshack. Grub time."

"Those are darlin' words to me ears," Patrick answered back.

Ten minutes later, a light knock sounded on the rear door of Philliphant's private car. Regis answered and ushered in Brendon Llewellyn, the chief engineer. Sterling Philliphant rose and extended his hand.

"Good to see you, Brendon. What can you tell me about these Indian raids?"

"Glad you're here, Sterling. As to the Cheyennes, I can't tell you a whole hell of a lot. They've hit us three times so far. No one killed, thank the Lord."

"The crazy devils attacked us, too. Shot up the sides of the cars, then pulled away and let us roll on down the track. Does that say anything to you?"

Llewellyn puckered his lips, pulled on his wide,

dimpled chin with a big, seamed hand. "Just warmin'
up for the big one, do you think?"

"It's a possibility. Here, sit down. Regis, would you
set out brandy and cigars, please? Brendon, have you
eaten?"

"Yes, I was finishing up when you pulled in. Brandy
sounds good."

"So, we may have a group of warriors whoopin' it up
to build their nerve for the final attack," Philliphant
enumerated. "Or we might have some young bucks
feeling their oats and just 'playing' at war. Then again,
they might have a real and determined purpose, but
don't want to start something that the Army would
finish with artillery and Gatling guns."

"That makes sense, Sterling. Only . . . which of the
three do we figure it is? And how do we act accord-
ingly?"

Chapter 11

Pinpoints of intense brightness flashed from highly polished buttons, bits and sabre hilts in the late afternoon sun. In a column of twos, the cavalry arrived at the railhead, with curb chains jingling and horses stepping proudly. Liam Daley looked up from his work and pushed the hat back on his head.

"All they need is a bloody brass band," he said nastily.

"The Army's here to protect us from those redskins," Sean O'Casey advised him. "I'd be for showin' a bit more gratitude, if I were you."

"Yer not me," Liam growled. "An' I think I can tend to me own protectin' better than those blue-bellies. So'jers have been used before to break up labor organizations."

"Aye. True enough. Only there's no such problems here. We don't have any unions. Save for the Brotherhood of Locomotive Firemen and the engineers' organization."

"Considerin' all the goin's on around here, mightn't it be a good idea to have some sort of brotherhood for our own protection?" Daley suggested tightly, though he gave Sean a wink.

"I'm in the Brotherhood of American Railroad Workers, Daley. Only right now, havin' a job at all is more important than that it be a union one. I'm grateful for what I've got, Injuns an' all. When ye work for the railroad, word gets around fast. There's lots of folks out of work back East. Most of 'em are like me. They'll take anything, so long as they have a way to feed their families. In conditions like that, sure an' ye don't go about talking organizin'."

"Ye might be right, Sean O'Casey. But if things get worse out here, there's na' else a man can do to protect hisself."

Daley moved away, with Sean looked speculatively after him. Bloody hell. Could this Liam Daley be a labor organizer? Sean didn't like that possibility at all. The soldiers had moved off a short way and started to set up camp. Two of them, and a tall feller in buckskins, walked toward the private car that had come in at noontime. Well, not for the likes of Sean O'Casey to speculate on them. There was lots of track to lay. He hefted his twelve pound mallet and bellowed for his roustabouts to get on back with a bucket of spikes.

"This is Chief Scout, Eli Holton, Mister Philliphant, Miss Philliphant," Captain David Roberts ended the introductions.

"Pleased to meet you. Pardon me for saying so, Mister Holten," Sterling Philliphant went on. "You seem a bit on the peaked side. Have you been ill?"

"Lung fever, the doctor said," Eli informed the railroad magnate.

"Ummm. A serious ailment, sir. I trust you have recovered fully?"

"Not actually. And there are some men who suffered exposure during the blizzard who need bed rest and more care," Eli supplied.

"How many are laid up, Captain Roberts?"

"Only four. Five, counting Eli. That won't interfere with our patrol activities, however."

"I'm relieved to hear that, Captain. When do you propose to start?"

"Tomorrow morning. Too late in the day now."

"Fine. Get your men settled in. They can eat in our mess car, if you wish."

"We brought along most of our own supplies. Some things, like fresh eggs, we'd be grateful for, if you can spare them."

"We have them by the case. Have your cook consult with ours and get what you need. And, it would be my pleasure to have you and Mister Holten, and Lieutenant Stone join my daughter and I for a late supper tonight."

"That's most kind of you, sir. Thank you."

"Now I must say that these raids by the Cheyenne are most disruptive. They've slowed us down by about a day and a half, according to my chief engineer. That's seven and a half miles of track. We wanted to reach the badlands by the onset of winter. Humph! I suppose that's out of the question after that blizzard. That put us another two days behind. It's the Indians, however, that you gentlemen are concerned with. Let me give you an overview of what has gone on so far."

Before the president of the line could begin his review, the steam whistle of the *General Stande Watti* hooted three times and the car jolted backward. Those standing staggered. Eli Holten caught hold of a chair to steady himself. Sterling Philliphant smiled with all the mischief of a small boy with a slingshot.

"I hope you gentlemen don't mind a short ride on the Platte River and Pacific. There's a 'Y' about a mile and a half down the track. It's a large loop with a special switch. Allows us to reverse direction without a round house. We'll go through it and back into position here

That'll allow the locomotive and empty flatcars to return to Omaha tomorrow morning. Now, then, where was I? Oh, yes. The raids. Everyone take a seat."

Carefully, concisely, Sterling Philliphant laid out the details of the Cheyenne attacks. He even had the exact name of every wounded man, his job assignment and the nature of his injury. After dealing with the human casualties, he paused in his narration to summon Regis, who dispensed brandy, cigars and a variety of light sweets. Gwen excused herself and stepped out on the observation platform. Then Philliphant launched into a description of the damage done to equipment and material. When he reached the end of the list, he sipped his brandy and began on a new tack.

"I've been thinking about this since Brendon here described it to me earlier. There is one significant fact in all these raids. Did you notice it, Captain? Mister Holten?"

Eli grinned broadly. Philliphant might own a railroad, but it didn't prevent him from using his brains. A glance at David Roberts gave him a consenting nod.

"So far," Eli began, "no one has been killed."

"Exactly. And where does that lead us?"

"Davey and I, Captain Roberts and I, discussed this on the route here. Most people out here allow as how I know considerable about Indians. A little background for your benefit and for Mister Llewellyn. I lived with the Oglala Sioux for nine years. I met a lot of Cheyenne. Neither tribe is noted for holding back in battle. The plains sign language symbol for the Sioux is a hand edge across the neck. Cutthroats. An equally unflattering sign denotes the Cheyenne."

Eli demonstrated by making a palm-down arc with his right hand, balling it into a fist and grinding it into his left. "It translates into something close to, 'They who come to kill.' Only this time they haven't done any

103

of that. In fact, from what you just said, Mister Philliphant, it appears they destroyed more property than they did damage to people. Which leads me to . . ."

"The same conclusion I've arrived at," Philliphant interrupted. "These Cheyenne are more interested in keeping the railroad out of their country than in starting a war with the whites."

"That's how Davey and I see it," Eli acknowledged.

"How do we proceed in light of that?"

"We find them, palaver over the matter, try to convince them that a war they don't want will come anyway if they don't return peacefully to their winter camps."

"Humm. That sort of thing is possible?"

"Oh, yes. It's a matter of timing. So long as they have killed no one, we can offer total amnesty in good faith. They've been lucky up to this point. Arrows don't always fly straight. A slight deviation and, no matter how careful the aim, the man intended to be wounded becomes a corpse."

"That's a grim prospect."

"One the Cheyenne probably don't take into consideration. Their war chief's *intention* may be to avoid any killing. Warriors tend to be totally individual, even when directed by someone else. It could happen anyway."

"And then?"

"Then, Mister Philliphant," Dave Roberts interjected, "the Army would have to step in and treat it as an act by hostiles. Hunt them down, round the survivors up and ship them off to Oklahoma. Indian Territory."

"Hummm. For the life of me, I can't exactly applaud that solution."

"Oh?" Eli inquired, loading the single word with

considerable meaning.

"I have nothing against the Indians. In fact, I'm rather somewhat *for* them. My idea, from the start, has been to develop a railroad that will help their people as well as our own. I don't want to become the cause of emnity at this point."

"You won't be. If they break the law, the blame is theirs. Our job is to see they don't. I'll be sending out patrols starting tomorrow, as I told you. When the camp is located, Eli and I will go there to open negotiations. We're not exactly a peace commission, but we can act for the Army and on your behalf."

"Excellent, Captain. You two don't impress me as dedicated Indian fighters. Perhaps, between the three of us, we can make the Cheyenne see reason."

"We can try."

The whistle hooted again and the cars jolted to a stop.

"We're at the switch," Philliphant informed everyone. "We go in and make the loop, which brings the train out with the engine facing east. Then reverse back to the rail head."

Another series of steamy blasts came and the rolling stock jolted into motion again. At barely five miles per hour, the walking beams of the drivers seemed hardly to move. The trucks of the cars creaked and groaned. A grinding sound came from the rails. A series of short, hurried toots came from the locomotive.

Brendon Llewellyn, who had been gazing out the window, turned with an expression of consternation on his face. "Indians again! It's the damned Cheyenne."

Gwen Philliphant, her eyes wide with astonishment, came rushing in from the observation platform. "They . . . they're attacking the locomotive. They have ropes along. I think they expect to pull the engine off the tracks."

No shots had been fired toward the cars. In light of this, the men crowded onto the rear platform and looked over a portion of the arc to the locomotive. Cheyenne warriors raced around and in front of the steam-spouting engine. Some launched arrows or discharged their rifles in the direction of the cab. Others, with ropes in hand, threw wide loops in an attempt to snare the big diamond smokestack.

"Look at that," Philliphant said with wonderment. "Do they actually think they can pull over forty five tons?"

"It don't matter what they think," Eli informed him. "It's what they believe. And what they get done."

First one, then another braided rawhide noose slipped over the wide top of the No. 4's black-belching smokestack. The braves who held the opposite ends rode swiftly away, at an angle perpendicular to the tracks. Swiftly the ropes went tight. Metal shrieked and groaned, wavered and then began to topple.

In a shower of soot and smoke, the diamond-shaped stack bent sideways and crashed to the ground. Hot sparks showered the air from the open pipe end. Without the spark catcher and clinker grinder built into the big upper portion, the ferocious draft of the boiler fire spouted glowing coals like an erupting volcano.

"Damn them!" Llewellyn shouted. He angrily shook his fist. "They've gone and done it. Now what?"

In answer, more Cheyenne ropers flashed in and dropped loops over the steam and sander domes. They, too, kicked heels into their ponies' ribs and rode swiftly away. A small return line broke and sprayed the area around the locomotive with raw steam. Metal made odd straining sounds, while bits of ornamental brass broke off and flew through the air. One rider found himself yanked from his pony's back, still holding his rope.

With less leverage, and tapered tops on the domes, the ropes eventually slid up and off. Eli Holten and the two army officers had their sidearms out and fired at the swarming mass of Cheyenne warriors. Eli spotted the leader, his feather-decorated lance raised high in preparation for another signal. Holten took careful aim.

The bullet from Eli's Remington .44 smacked into the hard wood of Spotted Horse's lance. It sent shivers of numbness through the war chief's fingers and jerked the long shaft from his hands. Instantly, he swept low and retrieved his fallen weapon. Then he hooted a shrill call for attention and directed his followers away from the stranded train. With Brendon Llewellyn's curses trailing them, they quickly galloped out of sight.

"Damn, damn, damn," Isaac Stone complained. "No way to alert our troops. This would be an ideal time to track them down."

"My feelings, too," David Roberts put in. "Mister Philliphant, will this train be able to return to the rail head? I'd like to send out a couple of men to trail that raiding party while the tracks are still fresh."

"Oh, we can make it, all right. Trouble is we'll be black as Pennsylvania coal miners from the smoke and soot. And, there's a chance of starting a fire."

Andrew McMahon appeared at the back of the group on the observation car. He caught Sterling Philliphant's attention and the railroad tycoon worked his way to the conductor.

"Mister Philliphant, do you want me to have Charlie signal trouble again? We can get some men here quick on handcars."

"Good idea. Do it."

Twenty minutes later, three handcars arrived, loaded with men, all heavily armed. Sterling Philliphant greeted them.

"Won't be any fighting, boys. What you'll need to do is get that smokestack on a flatcar, tie it down good. Then all but six of you walk the track while we back to the rail head. Make certain any sparks are put out. We sure don't want a fire."

Within ten minutes the task had been accomplished. Spouting a thick column of unrefined smoke and coals, the damaged *General Stande Wattie* began to build steam. Charlie leaned on the whistle and the drivers spun on the rails as he applied steam to the pistons. Slowly the train began to move.

Once the turn-around had been completed, the two officers returned to the private car with Philliphant and Llewellyn. Eli Holten remained on the observation platform with Gwen Philliphant. Now the "front" of the train, as it moved toward end-of-tracks, the roofed over vestibule remained free of gritty contaminants. Eli stepped up close beside Gwen and spoke in a deep, quiet tone.

"I'm not much of one for formalities, Miss Philliphant. May I address you as Gwen and you call me Eli?"

Gwen made a half turn, startled slightly by the scout's forwardness. "Why . . . um, certainly, Eli. Like Daddy, I couldn't help but notice you seemed only recently recovered from an illness. I hope your restoration is complete."

"It wasn't so debilitating as you might think," Eli deprecated. "I meant to compliment you, Gwen. You handled yourself quite well during that attack by the Cheyenne."

"You mean, no hysterics, no vapors? All of that?"

"I'm quite sure it would take more than a few yipping warriors to put you in hysterics, Gwen. As to vapors . . . you don't seem the type."

Gwen produced a small moué. "Why is that?"

"While we were eating, I overheard some of the men who came in on your train remarking on how you took charge when a cave-in buried two workers in a snowdrift."

"Railroaders have a habit of exaggerating things," Gwen deprecated.

"I think not this time. Whatever the case, I determined right then to get to know you better."

Gwen gave a close inspection to the man who addressed her. She admired his rugged build, the quiet aura of great strength and determination that even the ravages of lung fever could not erase. His gray eyes seemed to personify this vast, forbidding prairie. Curly blond hair, thick and lush, adorned his head and she found tingles of excitement coursing through her as her gaze rested on full, sensual lips. She smiled and he returned it.

"I . . . uh, think I would like that, Eli. Yes, I certainly would."

Chapter 12

Sparkling crystal and fine bone china covered the table in the dining room of Sterling Philliphant's private railroad car. Finely crafted Revere silver service shone up from flawlessly white tablecloth and napkins. Candles shed soft, yellow light. The dinner party atmosphere came to Eli Holten and the cavalry officers as a welcome relief from the hardships of the past week. It also served to bring Eli and Gwen into closer proximity.

"A decidedly pleasant prospect," Eli said softly as he considered the situation.

"Pardon?" Gwen, seated at his left inquired.

"Oh, uh, nothing. I was muttering to myself. I approve of the seating arrangements," Eli robbed the statement of presumption with a warm smile.

"So do I." Her eyes spoke boldly. Gwen bent toward Eli and continued in a conspiratorial whisper. "I do hope Regis managed to explain to those boys about how to serve at table."

"Eh? Which boys?"

"Two young lads on the work crew. Regis had no idea we'd be entertaining anyone but Brendon Llewellyn, so he didn't bring along any waiters. These boys are definitely make-do."

Sterling Philliphant broke off his conversation with Captain Roberts and Brendon Llewellyn to ring a small silver bell. Looking uncomfortable in stiffly starched white waiters' jackets, Timmy Pruett and Archie Boyne entered behind Regis, each bearing a large silver tray loaded with bowls of steaming clear broth. A bit awkwardly, they divided and went to opposite sides of the table. Regis began to distribute the soup course.

"Mister Holten," Philliphant addressed the scout. "Captain Roberts tells me that of the two assistants you have along, one is a Sioux. Is that common practice?"

"It certainly is. Though, Tommy Red Hawk is a half-breed. His father, Tom Jordan, runs a small trading post north and east of here. His mother is an Oglala. He's young, but he's learning and he does well. He, ah, is my nephew, since I was adopted by his mother's family when I lived in their village."

"Splendid!" the railroad baron enthused. "And it gives the young man an opportunity to learn our ways. Has his father given consideration to higher education?"

"It's a bit late for that. Tommy's nearly twenty."

"Never too late for a sound college education. The reason I mention it, I recently made a substantial, ah, endowment to Carlsyle Institute. It should be merely a formality were I to recommend him for admission."

"That's a considerate and generous offer, Mister Philliphant," Eli returned. "But, as I said, it's probably too late for Tommy. He can read a little and do sums up into the thousands, but he's never had a day of formal schooling."

Philliphant frowned slightly. "Things are certainly different out here."

"They are particularly when a boy spends half his

111

year at an isolated trading post and the remainder riding Sioux ponies and chasing buffalo. Tommy speaks Lakota, *Tsistsistis* and English. In that order of fluency."

"Eli," Gwen interrupted. "What is this *tsi-tsis* . . . ?"

"Cheyenne. That's the name they call themselves. It sort of means the Red People from the Hills. The Sioux call them *Sahiela*, which means, 'They Come Red.' Comes from the Cheyenne use of a lot of red paint and red dyes. The two tribes are related, distantly, and have been allies for more'n a hundred years." Eli turned his attention to Philliphant.

"That's why we're anxious to get this problem of yours solved. If some of the Sioux get the idea that it's fun to tear up railroads, we could have trouble from the Northern Pacific clear into Kansas."

"I appreciate the difficulty you face. To me, it's more personal and more immediate. However, if I can be of help in any way toward ending hostilities, please call on me."

"Be sure that we will, Mister Philliphant."

A loud clatter of falling pans in the kitchen interrupted conversation.

"Boy, you got ten thumbs," Regis' voice came muffled by distance. "Best be to holdin' onta things or I'll warm your behind with the flat of my cleaver."

Gwen made a face. "Oh, I just *knew* this idea wouldn't work."

"Now, my dear," Sterling Philliphant interceded. "They're only small boys. And Regis can manage, I'm sure. Captain Roberts, I hear from the rumor mill that you are about to become a married man. Is that so?"

"Eli!"

"Not me, Davey. I didn't say a word."

"When I find out . . ." Dave Roberts cut his ire short. "Uh, that's right, Mister Philliphant. A girl I've

112

known for some two years. She's a, uh, teacher in a small town east of here."

"Well, well. That is a good bit of news. I imagine it can get rather lonely out here without companionship."

"Oh, it does. Officers aren't encouraged to get married before they make captain, so life can be hard on many of them."

Regis, his face frozen to show no emotion, entered with the red-faced boys to remove the soup bowls and announce the main course. Each lad managed to deftly slip the empty plates away without undue clatter. They stacked them on the silver trays and departed toward the kitchen.

The remainder of the late supper went without noisy incident. Timmy and Archie learned quickly by repetition and managed not to drop anything else. Already the boys, only two years different in age, had formed a close friendship. Timmy had gotten Archie a bunk next to his on the top tier of the second dormitory car and introduced him to Sean O'Casey. Sean in turn had met Brian O'Dwyer and liked Archie's uncle. Now, impressed into this unusual employment, the youngsters helped each other and covered for their minor slips. When the men adjourned to the parlor section for brandy and cigars, the boys quickly cleared the remaining dishes and whispered together as they washed them.

"That Eli Holten is sure a big feller, ain't he?" Timmy asked his friend.

"He's that. Sure it 'tiz that I'd like to have done the things he has."

"Did you see those little wisps of black hair tied to the thongs of the buckskin shirt he wore this afternoon?"

"So? They look silly to me."

"Archie, I've lived out here longer than you. Each of

113

those represents a scalp he's taken."

"Mary and all the Saints! Yer funnin' me, ain't ye, Timmy?"

"Not a bit of it, Archie. I've seen lots of Sioux warriors. The last time the Oglala and Hunkpapa raided into Nebraska, I was four years old. Now there's peace, more or less. After Custer, those what wanted war moved north to Canada or west of here. The ones on the reservations aren't allowed to show off their scalps any more. So they wear those little slips of hair. Sort of like a soldier's decorations."

"Then, how'd Mister Eli Holten come to have 'em on his shirt?"

"Didn' ye hear him, Archie? He *lived* with the Sioux. Probably fought with 'em against enemies."

"White folk?"

Timmy shrugged and crinkled up his button nose. "I don't think so. Most likely the Pawnee and Crow. They're long-time enemies of the Sioux."

"How'd ye learn so much, Timmy?"

"By keepin' my ears open. Also we studied about it in school."

Archie's eyes widened. "Ye've been to a formal school now is it?"

"That I have. In Omaha. Near to six years of it."

"Sure an' yer an intelligent lad, then, Timmy. Meself had on'y two years in County Cork before we come to this country."

"You should be gettin' more schoolin', Archie."

"Poppa wanted me to. But this business crash came not long after we got here and there was never the money for it."

Regis appeared soundlessly behind them, fists clenched on his hips. "Y'all will get more work done if there's less talkin'. Y'hear me?"

"Uh . . . yessir, Mister Regis, uh, sir," Timmy

114

exclaimed breathlessly. He'd been startled by the sudden arrival. That was one *sneaky* darky.

Eli Holten remained behind after Dave Roberts and Winfield Stone departed along with Brendon Llewellyn. The scout stood with Gwen Philliphant on the observation platform. Silence held a long while as they took in the awesome panoply of the stars. During the quiet moments, Gwen moved closer to Eli.

"I've never seen them quite so clear. Even in Omaha there are so many lights. Why, there's millions that most people have never dreamed exist."

"It's funny. I've lived under all those since I was fifteen. After a while I sort of took them for granted. They're beautiful, though, aren't they?"

"Oh, yes. So many sizes and colors."

"There's a story among the Sioux that they are pebbles dropped by the Great Spirit — *Wakantanka* — when he shaped the earth. When he saw how pretty they made the night sky, he decided to leave them there to remind his children of his greatness."

"That's a wonderful legend. Are there many like that among the Indians?"

"Quite a few. About *Ptesanwin*, white buffalo-cow woman, who brought them their moral code. And Coyote, who's a trickster, *Miniwatu*, a water creature of old legends from when the Sioux lived around the Great Lakes. There's lots of them."

"I'd love to hear some."

"I'd like to spend a long time telling them to you."

"W-would you, Eli?"

"Of course, Gwen. You're a gracious hostess and a lovely young woman. What man wouldn't want to serve you? Gwenivere. It makes one think of the days of King Arthur."

"Lancelot and Gwenivere cuckolded Arthur, didn't they?" Gwen asked teasingly.

"So the story goes."

"And where do you think I see you among the knights of the Round Table?"

"Uh . . . as Galahad, perhaps?" he responded jokingly.

Gwen stepped closer to Eli and raised a small, warm hand, which she placed against his cheek. "No. As . . . Lancelot."

His illness had not permanently affected Eli's ability to respond. He'd felt a tightening in his loins the first time he saw Gwen Philliphant. The longer he was near the attractive young woman, the more intense his desire became. Her small delicate figure, creamy, angelic features and commanding blue eyes entranced him. She was tiny as a small girl, only some five foot three inches. It did nothing to dampen his ardor though.

Eli cleared his throat. "Er . . . Gwen, ah, I somehow get the impression you've been reading my mind. That is, I mean . . . no I *don't* mean that the way it sounds. Or, rather . ." Eli took command of his rambling thoughts.

"We've only met, Gwen and I'm embarrassed to say how strongly affected I am by your presence and your lovely appearance. I feel almost as though Fate ordained our acquaintance."

God, that's stuffy and stilted, Eli thought wretchedly. Then Gwen's question startled him anew.

"Do you believe in love at first sight?"

"No. That's a romantic notion thought up by spinster poets."

"I don't believe it either. But, there's always the chance . . ."

"That a second or third sight might improve mat-

116

ters?"

"Exactly. That or drive star-crossed lovers away from each other."

"Now, that's what I call cruel."

"I'm not a child, Eli. I'll be twenty before spring comes. I'm well aware of the wiles of suitors, especially those who have their eye on my father's wealth. You, though, are not one of those. Somehow I get the impression that you'd be less malleable than they."

Eli snorted slightly. "If you mean, would I leave the frontier and live in the lap of luxury off the largess of your father, the answer is decidedly no. I don't want to be Mister Gwen Philliphant. I'm not even prepared to say I have any desire to be married."

"What about your friend, Captain Roberts?"

"Davey needs it. He'll make a good husband and father. He deserves it, in fact. On the other hand, I'm set in my ways. I'm a loner. I . . ."

Gwen produced a pout. "Now you sound like you're doing your best to discourage yourself."

"Perhaps I am," Eli admitted with a grin. "Or to dissuade you."

"Why, Mister Holten, I declare, you've an abundance of affrontery to even suggest . . . even imagine . . . that . . . *I* have any such inclinations."

"Don't you? I know for certain that I do."

"*Eli!* You're atrocious. There's a difference between being bold and being brazen."

"Oh? Is there? I hadn't noticed the distinction in the past few minutes."

Gwen stamped one small foot, then turned on her heel. "*Good night*, Eli!"

She paused, watching him over one shoulder. "And here I'd made up my mind to kiss you. How could I ever have considered it?"

"Because you're attracted to me every bit as much as

I am to you. Forget your father's wealth, forget his railroad, forget his private car. It's you I'm madly taken by. You, you, you!"

A tinkle of laughter came from Gwen's lips as she turned back. "Oh, Eli, you're a nuisance, but a nice one. I won't forgive you. Not for now, at least. But I will see you tomorrow. You'll be staying in camp?"

"Yes. Doctor's orders. He wants me to give myself some rest."

"Then I'll be your nurse until you are able to go about your duties again. Sleep well and I'll see you after breakfast."

"Aren't you forgetting something?"

"What's that?"

"The kiss you promised to give me."

"You are impossible!"

She kissed him all the same.

With the coming of a pleasant dawn, two details set out from each company. One would patrol along the ballasted right of way westward, while the others followed diverging trails left by the Cheyennes. Gwen Philliphant stood beside Eli Holten as the soldiers departed.

"I hope we'll know something soon," the young woman declared.

"We won't know much for two or three days. The Cheyenne war camp will not be within a day's ride of here. Too easy to locate that way. So, it will take some doing."

"You wish you were going along, don't you, Eli?"

"You've caught me. Sure I do. That's my job. When they come back, nothing can stop me taking the second trip."

"Is that why so many men remained behind?"

118

"Not so many. Seven are on sick call. The rest are to protect the camp. There are only a dozen troopers fit for duty here. The others are on patrol."

"While they're gone, let's make the most of it, shall we? I'd like to take you up on telling those Sioux legends."

Eli grinned at her. "They're best told at night, around a fire."

"That could be arranged, couldn't it?"

"Not with the Cheyenne on the prowl. And not without incurring the wrath of your father. I do have an idea, though."

"What's that?"

"After the *General Stande Wattie* leaves for Omaha later this morning, we could take one of those handcars and go for a little ride."

Excitement colored Gwen's cheeks. She clapped her hands like a small girl with a new doll. "That's a marvelous idea. We could take along something to refresh ourselves with and roll down the tracks for miles." In an instant, Gwen sobered. "But what about your condition? Would that do any harm?"

"I think not. At least, I'm willing to gamble for the opportunity to be alone with you for a while."

"Hummm. That sounds remarkably like you have an ulterior motive."

Eli flashed her a white smile of reassurance. "I do."

Chapter 13

Ringing musically, steel hammers pounded spikes into the oak ties as the gandy dancers advanced the iron rails. Ahead of them, ballastmen dumped and tamped gravel, while the tie crews set their heavy timbers in place according to the surveyors' marks. A warm sun and slight breeze made the day pleasant. One could almost forget the recent blizzard, Eli Holten considered as he strode out of the military camp, toward the private car that squatted on the single ribbon of track.

Eli had slept well the previous night. Better than any time since leaving Fort Rawlins. He'd eaten the biggest breakfast since he came down with the lung fever. The pain in his chest had dulled to an occasional twinge and he no longer gurgled when he breathed. Over all, he felt fit and able. Particularly for the day's planned activities. A tour of the ground by handcar seemed a good way to familiarize himself with potential ambush spots, provided the present patrols failed to make contact before the Cheyenne attacked again. Holten reached his destination to find Gwen waiting for him.

"Good morning, again, Eli."

" 'Morning, Gwen. The train's on its way to Omaha and the day is ours."

"You sound mighty perky for a sick man," she

teased.

"Today I am a new man. I wanted to try talking Doc Lewis into letting me go. It wouldn't have worked, though. He's too stubborn." Eli paused to grin at her small frown. "Besides, I wanted to spend today with you too much to let a little thing like duty get in the way."

"I'll take that as a compliment, Eli. I'm ready to go. I had Mike Malloy set a handcar on the track after the *General Stande Wattie* pulled out."

"Then let's not waste time. Lead the way."

Gwen made a face. "I though you were the scout. Surely you can find the railroad track this close to it?"

"Enough, woman. You drive me to distraction."

Arm-in-arm, they walked the length of the elaborate personal car. Gwen carried a small basket. The pleasant aroma rising from the contents told Eli some of Regis' superb cooking rested inside. Hopefully nothing like an elaborate meal of the previous evening. The scout paused when they reached their conveyance.

Squat and wide, resting on four small wheels, with a central pillar that supported a teeter-totter type cross bar, the handcar resembled a bilge pump Eli had once seen on an ocean-going vessel, more than a piece of railroad equipment. He handed Gwen up onto the wooden platform and joined her. She stowed the basket against the base of the upright and reached for a long wooden handle through the end of the crosspiece.

"It's really quite simple, Eli. Once we get it rolling, we alternate pumping up and down on the handles. There's a connecting rod and cam system under the floor boards that turns gears to make the wheels work."

"You know quite a lot about these," Eli complimented.

"For a woman, you mean? Daddy made me learn everything about the operation of a railroad when he first started out. Earlier in fact. When he worked for the Pennsie and the New York Central, I had trains for toys and spent Saturdays in the yards with him. I could run a switch engine by the time I was twelve."

"Remarkable. What other dark secrets do you harbor, Gwen?"

"I'll tell you later, when we're away from so many ears." Gwen turned to six men who had come for another rail, their icetong-like tools ready to take a bite of steel. "Would two of you please give us a push to get started?"

"Right away, Miss Philliphant," one answered in a respectful tone.

The burly trackmen fell to with a will. Their legs churned and the light handcar began to roll down the track, its long propelling arm dripping and rising. Gwen clapped her hands in excitement.

"We're off!" she cried. Then she grasped the wooden handle and indicated Eli should do the same. "From here on, we do the work."

The little vehicle made good time. Before long the construction site, which Eli faced, dwindled too miniature structures. The rails, laid straight and flat as possible, still had to follow the natural contours of the land, so that within a mile, the small car dipped below a gentle swale and Eli lost sight entirely of the work train and water tower.

"How do we get this thing started to go back?"

"We don't. Or you can try alone. Now you know how, it shouldn't be to much difficulty. Doesn't it smell grand out here?"

"That it does. It's only the dead of winter when there's no sweet scent of sage or pine, something to perfume the air."

"Why, that's poetic, Eli," Gwen declared. "I didn't know you were a romantic."

"I'm not. At least, I don't see myself that way."

They rolled past the "Y" turnaround and on along the track. Their talk turned to personal things, growing more intimate as they progressed eastward.

"Tell me, Eli. When you were among the Sioux, did . . . did you have a wife?"

"No. I had my share of opportunities, but I never took a woman as wife."

"Do you mean you never, uh, knew a woman in all those years?"

Gwen blushed at her boldness and Eli felt gratitude, it assuaged his own embarrassment. "That's not exactly the same thing. I never married. Maybe we should leave it at that?"

"Perhaps that would be best. For my own part, I prefer to be candid. You said you were fifteen when you were adopted by the Oglala chief, Two Horns. By that time, I had known the meaning of love for two years. Do I shock you, Eli?"

"No. I've met my share of, ah, early blooming girls." Holten's thoughts hurtled back to the delightful twins, Beth and Bonny. "Most of them, when they grew older, seemed to have a more positive attitude about such matters than their sisters with a traditional upbringing."

Gwen laughed in a light tinkle. "You're trying to be a diplomat, Eli."

The warmth Eli had experienced when he joined Gwen that morning had grown to a raging fire. An expanding tightness in his groin confirmed his mounting passion. Of a sudden, he found it difficult to speak.

"Hardly diplomatic, Gwen. I'm trying to say that I've desired you from the first time I saw you. You do . . . wild things to a man."

"I'm glad to hear that. Most of the men I'm around are scared to death of my father. Or at least the power he holds. I never know if they notice me or not. What sort of 'wild things' do you mean?"

Eli locked her gaze with his and spoke in a deep, resonant voice. "For one, that I want to make delightful love with you right here and now."

"Here? On the handcar? Oh, Eli, I've never heard of such a thing."

"Say yes, or I'll not be able to stand it another moment."

"I . . . oh, what . . . ? Yes, Eli. Yes, yes, yes. I've not been able to take my eyes off you. You're so . . . everything."

They slowed the service car gradually and it came to a stop near the top of a rise that gave them a clear view in every direction. No chance of being surprised here. Eli stepped around the operating mechanism and took Gwen in his arms. Their lips met, urgent and alive. Gwen parted hers and opened her mouth at the probing of Eli's tongue. She pressed her lithe young body against his hard, unyielding one and shivered at the prominent evidence of his arousal. Breathless, they broke their embrace.

"Again," Gwen panted.

Eli gladly complied. His hands sought the firm, pert mounds of her breasts and began to knead them. Quickly her small nipples became tumescent. Gwen moaned and thrust her pelvis against the rigid fullness that swelled the scout's loins. She wrapped her arms around his neck and her fingers began to play about his ears and hair.

"Help me with my dress," Gwen requested when they ended their kiss.

Together they opened the fasteners, revealing Gwen's delightfully curvaceous body. Her creamy complexion seemed to glow. Eli pulled off his shirt while Gwen knelt and undid his trousers. She thought she would swoon at the massiveness of his rock-hard member. Never had she encountered one so large.

Truth to tell, there had been but few by which to judge. Her piano teacher, Professor Harmon, had initiated her into the secrets of love during the summer after her thirteenth birthday. His had been small, hardly more than a boy's, which she felt accounted for his preference for young girls. He had been patient and caring, moving her slow step by step toward the ultimate encounter.

When it at last happened, the marvelous sensations of pleasure it awakened in her drove off any thought of revealing their shameful secret to anyone. Gwen reveled in it. For the whole of summer and on into fall, each lesson, and there had been two a week, had ended in the creaky old bed of her instructor. It always left her desiring more. When the professor left Philadelphia for a responsible position at a music academy in New York, Gwen felt abandoned.

At least until she found herself being maneuvered into a compromising situation by a handsome boy in her neighborhood. Two years her senior, he seemed every bit as knowledgable and accomplished as Professor Harmon. And, to her immense delight, Virgil Downes had been better endowed than her music teacher. Their sharing of secret pleasure lasted for two years. After that she had only casual affairs with older men. They lacked any permanent involvement for either party. Only now. With this scarred, ruggedly handsome man, Eli Holten, she could not contain her excitement.

Gwen grasped Eli's bounty with both hands and drew it to her cheek. Heat radiated from his rigid staff. Gwen nuzzled it while Eli stroked her golden hair. She leaned back slightly and began to inscribe wet spirals on the broad, flat tip with her darting pink tongue. Eli grunted his appreciation.

Her gentle strokes inflamed the scout further. He bent and cupped hands under her arms. Slowly he drew her upright. They embraced and the world seemed to whirl for them both.

"Gwen, oh, Gwen, I want you. I need you so right now."

"Take me, Eli. Oh, be quick about it, before I lose my nerve."

"Why is that?"

"You're so . . . so *big*. I . . . I . . . Oooh! *Eli*!" Gwen cried out as Eli raised her slightly and guided her warm, moist cleft onto his pulsing phallus. Ever so slowly, he impaled her, trembling with the joy it brought him. His belly muscles grew rigid and star-bursts swirled in his head. Gwen whimpered and shivered with incredible ecstasy while she felt the bands of her passage stretched beyond all imagined dimension. She locked her legs around his waist and exploded into delirium as he began to rock back and forth.

After a seeming eternity, Gwen began to melt into the rapture of the most cataclysmic climax she had experienced since her first, induced at the tender age of thirteen. Weak, she clung to Eli's broad shoulders while he churned his way to his own oblivion.

"Oh, thank you, Eli, thank you, thank you," she panted as a new series of spasms wracked through her slender frame.

His moment of euphoria ended, Eli gently lowered her to the floor of the handcar. "I should be thanking you, Gwen. And I do. That's done me more good than all the medicine Doc Lewis carries. Now I know for sure I'm still alive."

"You're more than alive," Gwen observed as her light touch brought instant response from his semi-erect organ. "Oh, how *good* this is."

"Again? Ummm. Yes. Again and again."

Slowly the day drifted away.

Work continued at the railhead, supper still some hours away when the handcar returned. True to the promise Eli made himself, he took careful note of terrain features, with particular attention to covert routes of approach to the track and possible places from which an ambush of workmen or a train could be launched. He felt euphoric. Severely drained, tingly and muscle sore, he had become drowsy in the warm afternoon sun. Gwen had been more than a good partner. She had been astounding. Her soft, happy smile told him she, too, had shared in the bounty of their lovemaking. As they neared the camp, Eli noticed that the locomotive of the work train had steam up.

Of course, he reminded himself. End-of-track now extended some nine miles beyond the point where the Cheyenne had last attacked. Sterling Philliphant's private car had been hitched on to the rear of the string of dormitories and supply cars. If they worked hard, the handcar might catch up before the train moved. If not, they'd have a long, hard job of it. He pointed that out to Gwen.

"Oh, they'll wait," she replied confidently. "Daddy wouldn't leave me out here like that. Not with the Cheyenne raiding."

"He let you go off on a handcar with only me for protection," Eli stated the obvious.

"He had no idea how far we were going. He knows it's nine miles to the rail head. So, he'd not let the train move until we got back. You'll see."

Gwen's assurance proved correct. Sterling Philliphant waited on the observation platform while they drew near. A maintenance crew took over the small

127

hand-powered vehicle and Gwen said a quick good-by to Eli. His horse, Sonny, and that of Corporal Williams were all that remained at the cavalry camp. Everything else had been moved ahead.

"We'd better get going, Corporal," Eli advised.

Young and imaginative, the junior NCO replied with a bold and knowing grin. "Whatever you say, Mister Holten. She sure is pretty."

"That she is."

With lumbering slowness, the heavily laden work train slammed and clanked into life, then inched along the rails. It reached a slow walking pace of five miles an hour after more than twelve minutes had passed. Lost in pleasant remembrance of the day's amorous rich-ness, Eli took little note of the slow progress. He failed, also, to note an unnatural stillness. A coyote yip that had not quite the right tone to it caught his attention, though, a second before the Cheyenne attacked the train.

"Mister Holten, it's the Cheyenne!" Williams shouted.

"I'd already seen that," Eli answered as he drew his Winchester carbine.

A shiny brass round slid into the chamber and Eli brought the piece to his shoulder. He sighted on a red paint-splotched warrior near the front of the line of charging ponies and squeezed off a shot.

Flame spurted from the muzzle and the bullet cracked its way to the target. Impact of lead in flesh made a flat splatting sound. The brave reeled in the saddle and fell to one side. Only a random spatter of shots and moaning arrows erupted along the side of the train, while the bulk of the Cheyenne swept on toward the back end.

Too late, Eli Holten discovered their intention.

Five braves swung onto the front vestibule of the

128

Philliphants' private car. More streaked to the rear and leaped aboard from their mounts. Glass splintered and Eli heard Gwen scream. A shot blasted from inside. Eli began to fire rapidly into the swirling mass of warriors outside the moving car. A struggle developed at the rear doorway and three Cheyenne emerged, forcing Sterling Philliphant outward. Another trio came behind with Gwen.

Desperate, Eli fired at the abductors. One screamed and slammed back against the wall of the car. Eli fired again. For a moment, Gwen broke away. She started to dart back inside, only to be grabbed again and hurtled into the arms of a warrior on a piebald horse. Her father followed a second later into the hands of another waiting brave. Swiftly the Cheyenne galloped away.

Eli fired after them, as did Corporal Williams. Their resistance had little effect. Hopelessly, the scout had to watch while the president of the PR&PR, and the girl he had come to love so compellingly, disappeared into captivity with the whooping Cheyenne.

"Damn. Oh, damn, damnit all. Corporal, ride like hell to the new camp. The troops are still out, but a message has to be taken to them. I'll stay here and start marking the trail taken by those Cheyenne. We have to move fast or the Philliphants will be dead. And with them, any chance of a peaceful settlement."

Chapter 14

Dust still hung in the air from the surprise Cheyenne raid when Eli Holten started out in pursuit. Of necessity, his progress remained slow. With every change in direction, he left a marker, easily recognized by his fellow scouts, whom he knew would be along soon, leading the troops. All the while, his conscience gnawed on him.

Why hadn't he anticipated such a move? To which he could answer, why should he? After all, the Cheyenne had been harassing the railroad construction crew, not seriously attempting to kill them. Had they wished so, there would not be a man left alive. The certainty of this filled Eli's mind as he covered the miles of visible trail.

Then, on a stretch of slab rock, the raiders' sign disappeared entirely. Eli crossed the long table of bared sandstone and carefully examined the ground. Not a track. He found no clear sign to either side. For all purposes, it appeared as though the Cheyenne had vanished.

Here and there, he did find indications that something had been used to rub out hoofprints. If so, it had been done in a dozen places. He followed the most promising of these for some two miles. His respect for the war leader grew. Such diligence among fiercely independent warriors rarely occurred. Eli circled north and eastward, finding traces of the same determined effort. It would take the combined abilities of himself, Bill Fletcher and Tommy Red Hawk to unravel this deception. Resigned to this, he returned to the railhead, filled with disappointment and defeat.

"I don't know how we're gonna work it, Davey," Eli told his friend early the next morning.

"Nor I. We've ridden hard to get back here. The troops need rest, the horses more so."

"We can't wait, damnit," the scout snapped. "Every hour makes it worse for the Philliphants. It's my fault. I should have expected they would have men watching this place. When you rode out it was an open invitation."

"Don't kick yourself too hard, Eli. I should have left more men here."

"All right. So we share the blame," Holten agreed. "That still doesn't do anything for the Philliphants. Another thing. Now that this has happened, how can the issue be settled peacefully?"

Sean O'Casey turned a flinty stare on the man talking in low tones. Liam Daley returned the glare with an expression of icy insolence. A dozen men had gathered on the open floor of one dormitory car. Sean felt sure that one of these three dandies conducted a similar meeting in each of the other sleeping cars. The rhetoric was familiar to Sean. And he didn't like the tone of it.

"Sure now and the president of this fine line has got hisself captured by the hostiles. It's not safe, I tell yez, to be workin' for the Platte River an' Pacific. The army's fixin' to go harrin' off after the Injuns. What's that leave to protect us?"

"We did all right before," Sean countered when he saw the others reluctant to object. "What happened was that we got lazy, gave over the responsibility for protectin' our fine persons to the so'jer boys."

"That don't take away from the fact that we're likely to get our hair lifted at any time," Daley growled in answer. "What we need is a strong organization that can protect our lives *and* our rights."

Sean's eyes narrowed. " 'Rights' is it? What is it ye think we're bein' deprived of, bucko?"

"Why, damned near everything. The right to safe workin' conditions, for one. An' the right to hazard pay with these raids goin' on. Not to mention the right to a job at all."

"What do you mean by that?"

"O'Casey," Daley said in a friendly tone, "Ye've been out here a long time now. Things are changin'. What with this slump back East, money's tight. Right before we left for here, I heard talk that Philliphant was comin' out here to relieve all of ya of yer jobs. He's fixin to cut expenses by replacin' all ya loyal Hibernians with Chinese."

"No! That I can't believe."

"They work cheap," Daley declared shrewdly. "Ya can feed 'em on rice. They don't organize and they ain't got anywhere else to go for jobs."

"What ye say about the Chinkos is true enough, Daley. Only, I say that we're in no danger of losing our jobs. Even if ye've the right of it, what we should do is keep on workin', let the Army find Mister Philliphant and his daughter. Then we can ask him straight out."

These sharpers weren't on the level. Sean could tell that from the first day they arrived. Always complainin', castin' doubts to the four winds. What he'd like to know was exactly what they had hidden in their sleeves. He'd try to play on 'em to reveal their hand, he

132

decided.

"Brother Daley, supposin' we were to organize like you say we should? How would we be goin' about it? Are ye, perhaps, from the Brotherhood of American Railroad Workers?"

"No-o," Daley readily acknowledged.

"Then who would be behind us?"

"Well, uh . . ." Daley began to back down, uncertain how exactly to proceed.

"Listen boys. I don't know what our friend Daley here has in mind. He's not from the BARW, he said so hisself. An' I know it for a fact. I'm a member of the BARW, worked two union jobs back East. Sterling Philliphant has been good to us so far. He should be given the benefit of the doubt as far as this hirin' an' firin' goes. Talk about standin' up for our rights we're supposed to have lost, that's pure nonsense. As for organizin' for our protection from the hostile Cheyenne, that might be a good idea. For the rest, though, I think we should wait."

Heads nodded in agreement among the workmen. "Sean's right," Brian O'Dwyer spoke up. "Though we only got here, I ain't seen anything I can rightly say is bad workin' conditions, except for the Injuns." He got a chuckle for that.

"Why don't we hold off on all this until we see how the wind blows, eh?" Brian concluded.

"Sure. That's jake with me," another old-timer put in. "I've had worse jobs. Don't want to lose this one."

Fury flushed Liam Daley's cheeks as agreement went the rounds. He cast a deadly glare on Sean O'Casey and vowed to see the gandy dancer paid for this setback. The time would come.

Half of the troops, "C" Company, under the command of 1st Lt. Winfield Stone, remained at the railhead. Work continued as usual when the column of Dave Roberts' "D" Company, with the three scouts started out along the trail previously marked by Eli Holten.

"Here's where the trouble begins," Eli informed his fellow scouts and Dave when they reached the exposed rock slab. "For all you can tell, they sprouted wings and flew away."

"You mentioned indications of sign being rubbed out," Bill Fletcher reminded.

"Yeah, Bill. About a dozen places, going in all sorts of directions. Each of us will have to take a detail and spread out on the most likely ones. Somewhere they'll come back together."

"Then we have them," Tommy Red Hawk said as he slowly closed the fingers of one hand into a fist.

"We're not here to fight, Tommy," Eli reminded him. "We have to get the Philliphants back before anything else."

Ten minutes later, Eli set out with a detail commanded by Lt. Gordon Harris, with Sgt. Brian Chalmers along as NCOIC. The non-trail they followed led northward. Their journey continued until the sun rode high in the sky. Eli halted to give the horses a break and for the troops to consume a noon meal of dried, jerked beef, parched corn and cold coffee. The notion struck the scout that they might not be far wrong if they started a smoky fire and let the Cheyenne find them. He rejected the idea and proceeded according to plan.

By mid-afternoon, Holten had discovered the first unshod hoofprints. Only three horses, though he believed they followed a larger group. Perhaps a rear guard, satisfied now that no one followed? It could be. He pointed them out to Gordon Harris.

"See those, Gordon? Unshod ponies. Carrying light burdens. Could be youngsters left behind to watch the backtrail. Whatever the case, they're not moving fast. Must be satisfied the ruse worked."

"What says they're Cheyenne?"

"Nothing," the scout admitted. "There shouldn't be any Sioux around this area and we have been following the Cheyenne."

"Obviously. No wonder I overlooked it," Harris joked. "How long ago?"

"Ummm. That's one of the myths created by the writers of the dime novels. Best I can say is that they were made today. Edges are still crisp. It could have been an hour or five hours ago. Not more than that, I'd judge. All we can do is follow along."

"I'm for that. It makes me furious thinking about that pretty young woman in the hands of those savages."

"They haven't left a body behind, so they must be treating her fairly well. For 'savages,' as you put it."

"I'd think you'd be a bit more upset . . . considering . . ."

"I *am*, damnit. I still feel it was my fault this happened. Nothing for that, though. Let's get moving. We've been swinging further west for some time. I'm going to ride ahead a little and see where these tracks lead."

"Take a couple of troopers along to keep in touch."

"You're learning, Gordon. Good idea."

Holten selected three men. He left one soldier five hundred yards ahead of the column, with instructions to continue on, maintaining his distance. Another he left off a thousand yards further on. The last he kept with him as a messenger. The pair rode silently on through the rolling, brown grass of the prairie. An hour later, Eli and the trooper topped a rise some five

135

miles distant from Lt. Harris' column and saw in the valley below another platoon of D Company, resting beside a stream while their horses watered.

"We'll go down and find out what news they might have, then you ride back and notify the patrol."

At the creek, Eli was greeted by Lt. Ames. "I thought you headed off to the south," the scout remarked after shaking the officer's hand.

"We did. Didn't take long, though, before the trail started to swing west, then cut north. That Sioux breed of yours is a whiz-bang scout. He saw things where I swore there wasn't a bit to go on."

"Tommy's good, all right. Seems the Cheyenne are gathering. Might as well wait here until Harris joins up. We can camp for the night and move on in the morning. My guess is that Davey and the rest are somewhere ahead of us, trackin' right toward those low hills."

"Shouldn't we regroup before halting for the night?"

"No guarantee where the other track will cross these two. Daylight's a better time to push hard if we need to." Eli turned to the soldier who had accompanied him. "Head on back to the column and tell Lieutenant Harris to make all speed to this spot."

"Yes, sir, Mister Holten."

"Tomorrow, we should find those Cheyenne," Eli predicted confidently.

Groggy with sleep, Timmy Pruett responded to the noise beside him. He opened one eye and asked vaguely, "Where ya go'n?"

"Gotta take a leak, boy," Sean O'Casey whispered. "It's hardly a bit past midnight. Go back to sleep, lad."

"Unnf," Timmy replied.

Sean slipped quietly down from his bunk and walked

the length of the car. He opened the door carefully, so as not to awaken the labor-weary crewmen slumbering near-by. A chill in the air made him shiver, despite the longjohns he wore. Padding gingerly on bare feet, he walked a distance away from the track and fumbled at the front placket to free his penis and relive an over-loaded bladder.

A hissing stream splattered onto the ground and Sean sighed delightedly. Then he tensed. Had he heard a sound out there? He tried to adjust sleepy eyes to the darkness and peer beyond a screen of scrub brush. Yes. There. A darker form against the skyline. It moved again.

Bright, burning pain exploded in Sean's chest. What? What could it be? Another lance of agony ripped into muscle and sheered off bone. Oh, God, how it hurt. Sean struggled to find air to shout for help, only to fail.

Blackness engulfed him and he fell face-forward into the puddle of his foam-covered urine.

Chapter 15

Silence accompanied the faint light of breaking day at the railhead. Suddenly, a wail of inconsolable anguish shattered the quiet. Pale and thin, the sobbing of a child, it awakened the workmen to a new horror.

Intense pressure of an over-filled bladder brought Timmy Pruett out of deep slumber earlier than the usual clang of the triangle. He raised up and slid into his trousers, then donned his shoes. He noticed that Sean O'Casey's bunk was empty. Probably the same call of nature, the boy considered. He eased himself down from the bunk and worked his way silently to the door.

Outside the car, he walked off a short ways to relieve the insistent demand. As he opened his fly, his sleep-fogged eyes slowly focused on a huddled bundle some ten yards away. It looked like a drowsing man, wearing only longjohn bottoms. His mission forgotten, Timmy walked forward to find out.

It indeed proved to be a man. He lay in a tight ball, like an unborn babe, Timmy considered. Then he saw the pool of blood and glistening, sickly yellow-white of bone in a circle on the crown of the corpse's head. Timmy rolled over the body and recognized Sean O'Casey. Two arrows protruded from Sean's chest.

"Oh . . . Sean! Sean!" Timmy howled as he sank to

his knees beside his friend and benefactor. A distorted shriek of misery burst from the boy's lips.

Men came to the grief-filled summons. Their voices sounded far away to Timmy.

"What is it? Who's that?"

"Who shouted out here?"

"There, over there."

"My God, it's a man."

"What happened?"

"*He's dead!*" Timmy wailed. "Sean's dead." Tears streaked down his smooth cheeks and he shook in spasms of torment.

"Mother of God," Mike Malloy gusted out as he made the sign of the cross over the fallen railroader. "He's been done for with arrows. It's Injuns."

"Look, look," another workman shouted excitedly. "They lifted his hair."

"How'd this happen? Weren't the soldiers guarding last night?"

"Jesus! They'll come in an' kill us all!"

"What's going on here?" the gruff voice of Brendon Llewellyn cut through the pandemonium.

"It's Sean O'Casey, Mister Llewellyn. He musta come out in the night to answer the call. The Cheyenne got him," Mike Malloy explained. "Shot him with arrows and scalped him."

"Why, they've . . . they've never killed anyone before," the chief construction engineer gasped.

"They sure as hell have now," Arthur Lavin pointed out. Then he addressed the gathering number of workmen. "Men, this proves it's not safe working out here. At least until these Indians are dealt with. Even the Army's not protection enough."

Malloy knelt beside Timmy. He put one arm around the slender youngster's shoulders in a clumsy effort to comfort the child. While he did, he looked closely at

139

the arrow shafts.

"Red paint, yellow stripes on the fletchings. They're Cheyenne all right. God rest his soul."

"Come lad," Llewellyn said softly to Timmy. "There's naught you can do for him now."

"B-but he's my friend," Timmy pleaded, tears smeared on his face.

"We'll care for him right and proper. Best you go wash your face and gather yourself some."

Timmy couldn't walk. He staggered a pace then flung himself back across the dead corpse of his dearly loved companion. Brian O'Dwyer shouldered his way through the press and knelt beside the sobbing boy.

"Come, Timmy, lad. 'Tiz Brian O'Dwyer tellin' ye this. Come away. Sean's off to heaven with the angels and the saints now, me boy. There's not a thing ye can do for him. Come with me an' we'll ease yer sorrow. Me an' Archie."

Gently he lifted the grieving child and bore him away.

"By God, that ties it," Devon Flynn growled after Brian O'Dwyer's departure. "I for one say we ought to lay down our tools and demand better protection. Hell, even the president of the line isn't safe. Who's gonna die next?"

"He's right," a hesitant voice answered.

"Poor Sean. He was a good man. Maybe one of us could get it like that next time."

Mutters of unease rose among the men. Liam Daley added a new worry to the frightened workers.

"They could still be out there. Waitin' for us to bunch up like this. It could be a trap."

Quickly, the railroaders began to disperse. Belatedly, the awake-up alarm began to clang. The odor of brewing coffee and baking bread assailed the nostrils of the track and ballast crews. Few of them found it appetizing in light of the recent tragedy. As the work-men walked away, Brendon Llewellyn halted Mike Malloy with a gesture.

"I don't like this talk of a strike," the construction engineer declared.

"Me neither, Mister Llewellyn. Did you notice, it's those three fellers came in with the new men who are whippin' up most of the discontent?"

"I did. What do you know of them?"

"Not much. Two of them are gandy dancers, the other's your tally clerk."

"Find out everything you can."

"I'll do that, boss. You, uh, smell somethin' not quite right about this killin'?"

"Ummm, not exactly. At least nothing I can get hold of. Funny, though, how even Indians could get past the Army guards."

"They were Cheyenne arrows right enough."

"Hummm. And there's been a plenty of those around here of late. See what you can find. I'll be most interested."

"Right away, sir."

Shortly after sunrise, the door-flap of the squat, conical lodge that housed the Philliphants was thrown back by a boy who could hardly be more than thirteen. He gestured for Sterling and Gwen Philliphant to follow him. Once away from the tipi, he spoke rapidly in his own tongue, which neither white understood.

"You are to be honored. You break your fast with the chief this morning."

Their guide took them to another buffalo-hide lodge, where he reached out and scratched politely on the cover to announce their arrival. After a grunted re-mark from inside, the lad drew the flap aside and indicated that they should enter. Sterling Philliphant recognized the man he assumed to be the leader seated with three others at the back of the tipi.

"Welcome," Spotted Horse said in fair English. "I am called Spotted Horse in your language. Come, take your first meal with me. This is Bear Heart, my friend since we were little boys. Here is *Mist'aimahan'*, Owl Friend of the Dog Soldiers, and Eats-His-Horse."

"How do you do? I'm Sterling Philliphant and this is my daughter, Gwen. Why have we been taken captive like this?"

Spotted Horse quickly translated Philliphant's words. A staccato rattle of Cheyenne came from Owl Friend. "He says, 'why not?' You come on iron road in fancy rolling lodge. That makes you impor . . . uh, important."

How perceptive, Philliphant thought. "That's true. I'm president of the Platte River and Pacific."

"Humm. What does that mean?"

"Chief," the railroad magnate offered.

"Good!" Spotted Horse exploded. "No chief, no iron road."

"See here, that's not quite right. There are stock-holders, other principals. With or without me, the railroad will be built."

Shrewdness glittered in Spotted Horse's eyes. "I think that might be so. Or it might not. We'll see."

"You . . . you intend to kill us?" Philliphant asked with a quaver.

"Not . . . right away. We'll watch the iron road. If men stop, we let you go. That's . . . fair, isn't it?"

"You're the soul of diplomacy," Philliphant answered, despite the gnawing unease inside him.

"Sit. Food is coming. Woman's place is over there." Spotted Horse indicated a mound of buffalo robes, prepared on the opposite side of the circle of men.

Scowling, Gwen went to it.

A moment later, three boys began to bring in bowls of a thick gruel, followed by a smoking platter of roasted meat. Their host waved a hand expansively and helped himself to the viands. While he munched he began a long discourse with Sterling Philliphant.

"Long time now, there's much trouble between *Tsistsistas* and you whites. This land free. We ride where we want. Fight, hunt, raise children. Life's good for us. Then you *nia'tha* come. You've funny ways of doing things. Shoot, kill first, *then* talk peace. It is not true there was peace before shooting and killing?"

"I — I suppose there was," Philliphant allowed.

"Then, what's the reason to break peace to make peace? An honest man comes forward with an open hand. He's welcomed. He eats in the lodge of our people and he has our protection. If then he breaks the peace, he's shamed before all the people. There's great punishment for one so dishonorable. You see?"

"I'm beginning to understand. What is this? It's delicious," the president of PR&PR inquired after another slip of the gruel.

"Fat root — you call it potato — berries, sweet root, uh, onions. Good to warm your belly."

"Yes, it is. But, go on, please. I find this most interesting. Is your whole moral code so strict?"

"It must be so. Life is, uh, hard out here. Men who are truly free often can't agree on how to be good. Someone must show them the way. The war club and bow are our judges, our laws. A man is by, ah, nature loyal to his family, to his clan and his warrior society. Also to another who he has sworn to obey as war leader." Spotted Horse paused and looked meaningfully at Owl Friend.

"As a boy, he learns that he must obey the civil chief of his band, too. Those who do not follow all these

143

things, are outcasts. They're scorned by all good people. Is this not supposed to be so among your people?"

"Uh, yes, yes, it is. Though sometimes . . ." Philliphant paused, gathering his thoughts. "We are supposed to respect and abide by the laws of our society, and to render like to those of other peoples. Sometimes that isn't always the way it works out. We have our outcasts, too. In light of what you've said, how can we bring an end to the fighting between your people and my railroad?"

Spotted Horse thought a moment, while he chewed a succulent piece of roast elk. He licked his lips and reached for more before he began to speak.

"Let me tell you of how life was when I was a small boy. In doing so, there's a message for those who truly wish peace."

"Ummm. Go ahead. I hope I have wit enough to discover it."

"Always, many babies who are born to our people died before they had seen five summers. Those who survived had to be strong. When I grew old enough to be aware of things around me, the world seemed endless. We *Tsistsistas* roamed all this land. Even into the sacred Black Hills. Often we rode with our cousins, the Dakota. We would gather in the high summer for feasting and the sacred Sun Dance. Life was no less hard. But we laughed a lot. As I grew older, I swam and fished and hunted birds or rabbits with my friend Bear Heart and other boys. We danced together and played rough games. We worked, too.

"Buffalo wandered everywhere in big herds. Their numbers couldn't be counted. We made much meat. We feasted, we sang and laughed. White men were already here, though in small number. Mostly our people ignored them. Then, by the time of my thirteenth summer, when I went for my dreaming, hordes of *nia'tha* swarmed onto the plains.

"Soon the iron roads began to appear. Men who had been welcomed in our lodges started to kill the buffalo and leave the carcasses to rot. Their honor rotted with the dead animals, but it didn't matter much to us. Our people began to hunger and we didn't laugh so much. More whites came.

"They continued to build and to make dirt lodges. The soldiers came and told us we had to move to a place far to the south. The tracks to the south, and those to the north, have already cut the herds into small, separate bands. Our people hungered more. And we stopped laughing at all." Spotted Horse stopped his narrative and scowled at his guests.

"Another iron road will only make this worse. Soon there'll be no more hunting. What can we do then?"

"Odd that you should mention the very thing I described to one of our stockholders. I'm aware of the privation caused by the loss of your buffalo herds. Yet, there is always beef cattle, like we eat."

"The stinking meat," Spotted Horse declared in disgust.

Sterling Philliphant had never heard beef described as such and it aroused his curiosity. "How do you mean, 'stinking?' "

"Many days go by before a buffalo carcass begins to smell bad. It is enough to dry meat for winter use. Your, ah, cattle do not last in summer's heat long enough to cure properly."

"There's salt."

"If we have any. Did you see the message in my words?"

"I . . . think I did. That true freedom, as you knew it, can't survive when two such different cultures clash, is that it?"

145

"You have much wisdom."

"Then . . . you feel that there can never be peace between us?"

"That's . . . not necessarily so. We learn. So does the white man. As a boy I saw whites who were good. I see the same today. It costs nothing to talk. If something good comes from that talk, it's worthwhile. All things shall come as the Great Spirit wills."

The impassioned disclosure left Sterling and Gwen Philliphant with dwindling hope. A moment later, Spotted Horse signed that the meal was over.

"Come back. We talk again. You're wise and, I think, fair."

Sterling Philliphant left the meal feeling terribly unsure of himself.

Chapter 16

Flies buzzed irritatingly in the hot mid-afternoon sun. Devil's darning needles flitted their dual pairs of wings, made iridescent by the golden rays, swooping off in search of water. A stiff southwesterly breeze agitated the long, sun-browned prairie grass, which broke like waves around a reef where five men waited with a wagon and spare mounts. Their leader, a tall, burly man with a striking red beard, removed a large, floppy hat and mopped at his sweaty brow with a wide, hairy forearm.

"He's takin' his goddamned time," Luke Partridge growled.

"No doubt he'll be here, though," a prim, schoolmasterish man on the wagon seat replied.

Luke sneered. What the hell had they been saddled with this sissy for? Considerin' the job they had to do . . . well, he just might get his head busted open before it was all over. Percival Throckmorton hardly fitted the role he had been selected to play. This sort of thing always got to the rough and tumble. Men objected, turning stubborn and had to be convinced. What would Percy do? Hit them with his purse? Still, Percy was supposed to be an absolute wizard with blasting powder.

"Why the hell did we have to meet clear out here?" another hardcase demanded.

"Because we're not supposed to be connected with the others," Luke explained. "We go in, sign on to work and take it from there."

"Someone coming, Luke," Ned McKeon announced.

"I see 'em, Ned. You've got good eyes."

"Just so I don't get one knocked outta my head in this deal."

"You won't."

"I don't like it," Percy complained. "Sitting out here is just inviting some nasty Indian brutes to come along and scalp us all."

"Pull a loop around that kinda shit, Percy-boy," Luke snarled. "That has to be our contact ridin' this way now. By night-fall we should be safe and sound with the so'jer boys to protect us."

"*Mierda!*" Rincón spat. "How did I ever get talked into this. I don't know nothing about foking railroads."

The runty, hard-eyed Mexican, who hailed from Santa Fe, had been recruited at a small trading post a few miles inside Dakota Territory. He had only one name, which he pronounced with a long "O" so that it sounded like *ring-cone*, and a nasty disposition. He claimed to be on his way to the goldfields around Deadwood City. Luke figured Rincón to be on the dodge from the law further south. All the same, he'd do. Rincón liked to use a knife. And he had another thing in his favor, by Luke's lights.

He absolutely despised effeminate men. He referred to Percy as, "that *pinché puto*." Luke would cut a lot of slack for a sideman like that. What still stung was that Luke didn't know exactly what they had been sent to do. He'd find out soon. The man on the roan horse grew closer with each passing minute.

"You're the boys sent out from K C?" the hard-faced

stranger demanded by way of greeting when he arrived.

"We are," Luke responded, equally tough.

"I'm Liam Daley. We've got a lot to talk about."

"There it is," Eli Holten breathed out in barely a whisper.

"Oh, my God," Gordon Harris muttered.

The scout and the young cavalry officer, along with a single trooper, had been following the gravel banks of this deep watercourse for over an hour. The rest of the platoon waited some five miles distant. The remainder of the troops, under Capt. Dave Roberts and Sgt. Brian Chalmers had turned back for the railhead. Now the bold pair peered through the low-cropped buffalo grass, across a rolling stretch of prairie at the squat lodges of the Cheyenne war camp. A quick count confirmed twenty-eight short tipis.

"You figure two, maybe three warriors to a lodge," Eli instructed Lt. Harris, "that's fifty-six to eighty-four hostiles."

"Jesus Christ! They outnumber the company by nearly two to one. If we have to attack them out here in the open, we won't have a chance."

"If it comes to a shootin' war, Lieutenant Stone's company will be along, and we have that little field piece back at the railroad," Eli informed him.

"What do we do now?"

"We're here and so are the Cheyenne. There's little reason to delay. Send that private back and have Delaney bring up your platoon, just in case we need a little cover fire."

"Then what?"

"When they get here, you and I are going in and talk with the leader."

149

"Oh, shit!"

All the same, Lt. Harris complied. It would mean a loss of two hours while the soldiers maneuvered into place. During the interim, worry would not leave Harris' mind.

"What if some kids come down to swim?"

"Won't be any with a war party," Holten assured him.

"The warriors, then?"

"They'll have a lot else to keep them busy, I imagine."

Harris decided on another quick look at the camp. He raised up cautiously and peered across some hundred yards . . . directly at a cluster of five slender, nearly naked boys, all barely into their teens, who walked with determination toward where he and Holten waited.

"Thought you said there'd not be any youngun's along. There's a handful of boys, maybe twelve to fourteen comin' right toward us."

"Damn. Apprentice warriors are what they are. Boys judged ready enough to go on their first war path. That don't make 'em any less dangerous. We'd better wipe out our tracks and pull back a way."

Beyond two snaking bends, the scouts decided they had come far enough. He hunkered down, hand over Sonny's muzzle, to keep the Morgan stallion from snorting in reaction to the scent or sound of the Indian youths. From upstream, he and Harris could hear the shrill yells and peals of laughter as the Cheyenne boys sported about in the cool water. Memories of his years in the Oglala camp of Two Bulls flooded back on Eli.

From the age of seven or so, every Oglala boy knew how to swim. Throughout the summer they would take every chance to run to the nearest source of water and leap in with wild abandon. Even the older youngsters, those who had won a dream-seeker's loin cloth, loved to throw aside their scant clothing and join younger brothers in the rough-and-tumble play. Although senior to most of those who participated in the free-for-alls, Eli often found the attraction of refreshment from the heat and dust too alluring to resist. To his surprise and pleasure it had eased his acceptance into the band.

Unlike their white counterparts, the Sioux didn't consider it unmanly for an adult to join in childrens' games. Particularly when it involved riding horses or water. Eli had even seen proud, haughty warriors who bore the red paint slash marks on their arms to denote up to a dozen wounds, and whose scalp hoops bristled with twice that many tokens of victory, eagerly enter a mud fight with boys of eleven and under. When occasionally struck with the "magic" mud ball—one with a rock buried in the center—they would fall down laughing, while the children gathered around shrieking with delight. How different from many white families he had observed, where any part of the naked body was considered sinful, fun was condemned as irreligious, and it seemed beneath the dignity of the father to even deign to notice his progeny.

"How long do you figure they'll be there?" Harris' question dissolved the scout's reverie.

"Uh . . . hard to tell. Most likely not more than an hour. We don't have to go back, after all. Once the troops get here, we can ride out of the creek bed right here and go on in."

"I don't know how much I'm gonna like this."

"I'm not exactly aquiver with expectation," Eli admitted dryly. "Do you have something to use as a white flag?"

"Ummm. Just my shirt. Or my longjohns."

"You can do without somethin' inside your pants better than ride in representing the Army with a bare

151

chest. Skin outta 'em, and we'll tear off a strip."

"Tear them? They're the only pair I have with me."

"You'll get used to it."

Camp discipline must be more lax than usual, Holten decided when the soldiers arrived and the boys had not yet been called back to duty with the horse herd. He had worked his way back along the creek to prevent any untoward noise betraying the presence of so many soldiers. Now that he had guided the platoon into position, there remained only for he and Lt. Harris to show themselves and ride into the circle of lodges.

"I think I'll live to regret this," Gordon Harris muttered.

"You'd better hope you live to regret it in leisure," Eli amended.

At first, no one in the warrior village noticed the slow approach of two white men on prancing horses. Eli and Gordon got to within fifty yards of the encampment before one of the busily working braves called out an alarm. Spotted Horse, who sat cleaning and oiling his prized Winchester Model 68, rose to his feet and walked outside his lodge.

"What are white men coming here for?" he demanded of the men near him.

"We thought that you would know, Spotted Horse," Black Bear reposted.

"They carry a banner of peace," Eats-His-Horse declared.

"Huh. They come to barter for the iron road man and his daughter," Spotted Horse immediately assumed correctly.

"We will not give them up," Owl Friend stated decisively.

"Yet, I think it wise to listen to what they say," Spotted Horse countered. With arms crossed, he stood and awaited his visitors.

While the two slowly approached, he studied them. The soldier he dismissed at once. Merely a number among many numbers. The man in buckskin intrigued him. Once the pair had come close enough to distinguish features, this one seemed familiar, like a face recalled from the distant past. Older now, yet familiar.

When they halted in front of the war leader's lodge, the tall, yellow-haired man in buckskin frowned in concentration, then spoke in strangely accented Cheyenne.

"Spotted Horse?"

The Cheyenne's eyes widened as recognition came. "Tall Bear of the Oglala?"

"Yes. You remembered."

"So did you, only sooner than I. Why have you come?"

"You should know that, Spotted Horse." Hampered by his imperfect knowledge of the language, Eli Holten changed to Lakota as he and Harris dismounted. "We would see this war with the iron road ended."

"You ride with the iron road now?"

"No. I am with the Army."

"Why do the pony soldiers do the bidding of the iron road people?"

"We're here for their protection."

A taunting smile illuminated Spotted Horse's face. "Did you protect them when we bent the iron ribbons? When we burned the flat-sided logs? When we set fire to the water lodge? Or when we pulled the smoking snout from the iron horse?"

Eli translated for Gordon and answered ruefully. "You have the better of us there. Our protection wasn't much, was it? Not even when you stole the man who

153

owns the iron road and his daughter."

Spotted Horse laughed heartily. "That was a good joke, wasn't it?"

"Yes. Something we didn't expect. It showed good planning. All of your raids have been brilliant. Tell me, then, why is it that not a single white man has been killed? You did all these things, yet spared the lives of the men shooting at you."

A long silence followed. Spotted Horse looked at the scout with a crafty gleam in his eye. How much did he dare say?

"All of the people know that to kill a white man is to invite war with the soldiers."

"That is true. The same could be said for destroying whites' property."

Frowning, Spotted Horse found himself compelled to reveal the heart of his plan. "Some risk had to be taken. The iron road must be stopped. Those of our people who remain in this land do not want the iron bands to divide the ground. This is a bad thing that can't be allowed."

"What about stealing away the chief of the iron road and his daughter? That is far worse in the eyes of whites than burning some wood and bending rails."

Spotted Horse produced a sly smile. "What you say is true. Though now, we have something to bargain with."

Holten and Harris exchanged significant looks when the scout translated this. "Clever devil, isn't he?" the young officer remarked.

"More than that. He has us by the short hairs and he knows it. I'm going to try to set up a pow-wow." To Spotted Horse, Holten said in Lakota, "Everyone involved is here; the iron road chief, you, the Army. Can't we sit down and talk about this?"

"Does Phil'pant speak with a straight tongue when

154

he says he respects my people?"

Eli Holten's eyebrows rose in surprise. During the time he and Spotted Horse had been teenagers, the Cheyenne had learned English. It was certain that Philliphant didn't speak Cheyenne. This put a new light on matters. The scout nodded thoughtfully.

"Yes. I believe him. Do you know of the Carlsyle Institute?"

"A school to make *nia'tha* out of *Tsistsistas* boys?"

"Not exactly. Close enough, though, I'd suppose. Well, misguided or not, Mister Philliphant donated a lot of money to the school to help teach those of the People who wanted to go. He *does* respect you. We'll all listen and speak our hearts to you. Is it agreed?"

"It's . . . it's what I wanted," Spotted Horse admitted. "When the sun is high next time, come. We'll talk."

Holten gusted out a heavy sigh and nodded. "Good. We will be here."

Without a parting salutation, the scout led Lt. Harris away from the Cheyenne camp. He had other, alternative plans to discuss before any such meeting.

Whoever held the king and queen controlled the game. Eli Holten wanted a chance to recover those valuable pieces.

Chapter 17

In the privacy of their small encampment, Eli Holten and Gordon Harris talked late into the setting sun. Eli first laid out the course to follow in the meeting the next day. Then he approached his alternative plan.

"There's no question that whoever has the Philliphants holds the winning hand," Eli began by way of explanation. "Spotted Horse has the trumps now. I'd like a chance at getting them out of there."

"Humm. You two acted like you knew each other," Harris injected speculatively.

"We do. Spotted Horse and I did our first Sun Dance together."

"Your 'first?' "

"Yes. That was only what the Dakota call the *wambli wacipi*, the eagle dance. The golden eagle, when it's immature, is spotted with brown dots for camouflage. The Lakota name for it is *wambli gleska*. The dance is for boys who want to test their courage. I was seventeen. Spotted Horse was eleven. We were among the last three to drop to the ground. It earned us our first eagle feather."

"My God! Those, uh, scars on your chest . . . was that part of it?"

"No. That came later, when I pledged my word by a

promise to dance in the *wiwanyag wacipi*, the sun gazing."

"No wonder they say around the fort that you know more about Indians than any other scout. Living with them like that. I . . ." Harris cut off his remarks and returned to the subject. "How could we possibly get an old man and a girl away from so many hostiles?"

"First off, they aren't particularly hostile. They're a little angry, but not out for blood, remember? Had we a chance to talk to Philliphant before, it could be done tonight. As it is, I want to slip into the circle about two in the morning, locate them and let them know what we intend. If circumstances don't let us do it then, we can be ready following the meeting tomorrow. We need an alternative. Some plan we can fall back on without delay in the event we have no luck talking Spotted Horse and his advisors out of their purpose."

"It still sounds impossible."

"With luck I can do it and be back here by three in the morning, four at latest."

"You'll need a whole hell of a lot of luck to do that."

Holten looked levelly at the young lieutenant. "I know it."

"It's settled then, is it?" Liam Daley said in a low, intense voice.

Gathered close around, a dozen men nodded somberly. Devon Flynn released a pent-up sigh. They'd come this far. By this time tomorrow, there'll be a strike for certain sure.

"Who is it that will be representing us?" a dissenter inquired.

"Eye-crew," Arthur Lavin answered, using the acronyn. "The International Collective of Railway Workers. Oh, we're large in Europe and Canada. The railroads are all *organized* there," he glibly lied.

"And each of us is to get twelve more men lined up? That's near to the whole work gang."

"More than enough to call for a strike vote," Lavin assured him. "But it's more important to be sure of the men you recruit, than to fill the quota. Actually, all we need is a bit more than half. It would be nice, though, if it were to be unanimous. Then what chance would the bosses and foremen stand?"

"What about foremen? There's a couple who could help us sway the men."

"Naw," Daley replied. "They always side with the big-shots. This is a workers' rebellion against intol . . . uh, intolerable conditions. We don't need any toadies."

"Well said, Brother Liam," Lavin praised. "Now, you all know what to do. Tomorrow at the noon meal we'll take your reports and give you your assignments. From this point, you're workin' for ICRW. Good luck."

"I'm not so certain this is the right way to go about it. But I can't abide what's been happenin' to us, either. You can count on me."

"Thank you, Finnegan," Lavin declared warmly, while he gave the leadman of the number one track crew an affectionate pat on the shoulder. "We knew we could trust you to see the justice of this thing. Everyone get busy. I want to hear we have a full gross of determined men to back us by noon tomorrow."

A single drum throbbed in the circle of Cheyenne lodges. Off at a distance, a solitary reed flute sounded the notes of a song that reminded the player of his distant love. The fires burned low, except in the dwelling of Spotted Horse. There, Sterling and Gwen Philliphant had joined their captor-host for the evening meal. With the passing of the hours, the conversation had grown serious.

"There are not many Cheyenne, uh, *Tsistsistas*, in the north," Sterling observed.

"That is true. Some day the others will come back. They don't like that place in the south. It's hot and dry. Sand and cactus, little game to hunt. The children sicken and die. Soon they will return to their rightful land."

"Well then . . . uh, there is a reservation here?"

"Yes. Few live there. Mostly old ones who escaped the soldiers when they took our people south."

"All the more interesting. My railroad can benefit them, too, you know."

Spotted Horse looked doubtful. "How is that? The steam horses drive away the buffalo. If we all lived on the reservation we would starve."

"Not at all, my friend," Philliphant went on expansively. "The right-of-way would pass through what the government in Washington considers the Cheyenne reservation. You could get a lot of good from that. Think about this. What else, besides people, do the, ah, rolling lodges carry?"

Wrinkles formed on Spotted Horse's forehead. He worried the proposition around for a while, speaking vaguely while he did. "Horses . . . soldiers . . . the stinking meat—cattle—maybe other things?"

"Right. Your designated rations, supplies, farm equipment, all the things you need to survive on the reservation, can be brought directly there on my railroad."

"Agency people often steal what is supposed to be ours."

"I'm aware of that. But they don't do so right in front of you, in plain sight. When the train comes, what is taken off can be counted by your people. They will know what is to be theirs."

159

Gwen Philliphant wanted to say something, anything, to aid her father's argument. She remained silent, however. Although given the greatest latitude in joining adult conversations as a child, she had learned quickly enough that in this Cheyenne camp, a woman's place was to remain silent while the men made decisions. It rankled, but she had no choice.

"My mother, my father . . . they are old. They live at the Agency. Often they are cold, hungry, always they are angry at the greed of the white agent. Your railroad," Spotted Horse tried the new word. "The railroad will stop all of this?"

"Not entirely. At least not until you have men who can read the white man's words and know his system of numbers. Our baggage clerks and conductors have pieces of paper with marks on them that tell what is being left off and how much of it. A copy goes to the agent. Another could be given to one of your people. They would know for certain if there has been any cheating."

Spotted Horse reflected again on the faces of his aged parents. He thought also of all the others he had seen on Dakota reservations. Would this be a true thing? Could his people really benefit from the railroad?

"We will talk of this another time. Now, let me tell you of how we used to hunt the buffalo when their numbers blackened the whole prairie."

Frightened to the point he believed he dare not breathe, little Timmy Pruett remained squeezed down behind the tall stack of firewood for the heating stone in the end dormitory car. He had come there to grieve for his lost friend, Sean O'Casey. Timmy didn't like the other workers to see him cry. His heart ached and he

160

could hardly visualize anything through the long day except the kindly, smiling face of the dead gandy dancer. He ate sparingly at every meal and used his blankets at night to muffle further sobs. Somehow, he felt like an orphan. Now fear had replaced sorrow. What could he do? He trembled as the men spoke again.

"I don't trust that damned Finnegan," Liam Daley growled. He and Devon Flynn had remained behind with Arthur Lavin when the meeting of strike organizers broke up.

"He'll do as we say . . . or there'll be another death around here," Lavin replied coldly. "Are our disrupters set up all right?"

"Fit as a fiddle," Liam assured his boss. "What with the injuries an' all, we had no trouble gettin' 'em signed on."

"Excellent. They know what to do in the event there's resistance?"

"Sure an' that's a fact. Most of 'em have been through it before. Only two new lads. They're mean and tough and they'll learn fast enough."

"Then I think we're ready to start our strike."

"We make examples of anyone who refuses to quit work?"

"You make an example of the first one who doesn't walk off and go on from there. By tomorrow evening, I don't want anyone lifting a hand, except the cooks. With these five hardcases, we can be sure there'll be plenty of violence if the hold-outs try to band together with the bosses."

"Ye've a keen mind for details, Arthur," Devon Flynn praised.

"See that you keep your own minds on what has to be done," Arthur Lavin snapped back. "Now, get out there and help these morons line up the workers."

161

Fear like none he had ever known gripped Timmy Pruett after the three men departed. For a while he thought he might wet his pants. Then he got control of his shaking and wearily crawled from behind the stack of cordwood. Timmy didn't know exactly what they had been talking about. What was a strike? He'd have to take this to Mister Llewellyn. It had to be important.

Chapter 18

Wisps of misty white swirled in the wake of the scout's footsteps as he stealthily approached the Cheyenne war camp. A quirk of nature, caused by the sunheated ground and the chill October night air, produced a wooly, ten foot layer of fog to hug the prairie. Eli Holten harbored considerable gratitude for the advantage it gave him on this risky mission.

He had chosen to go alone. Exerting his new-found confidence, Lt. Harris had disagreed. In the end, Eli had consented to take Corporal Delaney along, at least to the edge of the collection of lodges. The pair worked well together, as they had done in the past. They soon reached the circle of squat tipis, where the scout halted his partner with a touch on his arm.

"Wait here, Corporal," he whispered directly into Delaney's ear. "I have no idea how long it will take. If you don't hear any noise, stand fast until I get back. Any disturbance, and you head back to let the lieutenant know I've been taken."

"Right, Mister Holten. It'll be up to him to figure out what to do next, eh?"

"He'd better call for reinforcements."

"My thoughts, exactly. Good luck."

Holten disappeared in the thick vapor. The whole camp lay in slumber. His first, and hardest, task would be to find the Philliphants. Logic indicated that they would be close to Spotted Horse's lodge. Cautiously, moving like a wraith through the whirling mist, Eli worked his way toward the central tent. To which side would they be? Not a horse snorted at his passage, their ability to scent a stranger dampened by the moisture in the air. He reached his goal with unusual ease.

Five lodges, Spotted Horse's being the largest and central, formed a half-circle in the middle of the encampment. Which one would house father and daughter? Eli's knowledge of tribal custom guided his decision. Silent on moccasin-clad feet, he tip-toed to the tipi on the right of the main one. Cautiously he eased up the door flap.

Three figures lay inside, asleep. None of them female and none a white man. Holten replaced the cover and moved one lodge to the right. He repeated his previous action. A solitary individual drowsed restlessly. Eli risked entry to identify the person. No alarm came. He bent low over the tossing sleeper.

Sterling Philliphant. Good. Only, where was Gwen?

Holten placed a hand over the man's mouth and whispered urgently into his ear. "Quiet. It's Eli Holten. I've come to help you get away from here."

"Ummmf." Philliphant thrashed a moment, then calmed and nodded to indicate he understood.

"Where's your daughter?" the scout inquired.

"The other side of the big tipi. The first one, I think. They separated us tonight for some reason. How can you possibly get us out of this?"

"Not easily. With this fog, I'm tempted to try tonight. Would you be able to do so?"

"Yes," the railroad president replied in a tone of reluctance. "Though I don't know if it would be to my best advantage to do so."

"Why's that?"

"I seem to have struck some chord of responsiveness in Spotted Horse. His parents live on that so-called reservation west of here. He likes the idea of preventing any cheating on the part of the agent. I think I've got him convinced the railroad could insure that. You know more about their customs than I. How would it look if I escaped after bending his attitude enough that he took away our guards?"

"Hummm. You've a point, I have to admit. Discourtesy is one of the cardinal sins among the plains tribes. All right. We stick to my original plan. It calls for you and your daughter to be edged into a position where you can slip from the village in the event our meeting tomorrow doesn't end the way we want. Once out of here, you can join the remainder of the patrol in that creek bed to the west. From there it should be easy."

"Until they discover we're gone."

"That we'll have to deal with when it happens. I had better alert Gwen. Get what sleep you can. You'll need the benefit of resting now for what'll come later."

"Thank you, Mister Holten. What if we reach an agreement with Spotted Horse?"

"Then there won't be any reason for you to escape. You can ride out with us."

"Let's pray that's the way it happens. Good night to you, sir."

Swiftly now, Holten worked his way to the indicated lodge. Again he found no guard outside. Nor one within. Gwen lay on a pad of buffalo robes, unfettered and restless like her father. He crossed to her in two strides and knelt beside her shoulder. Once more he put a hand out to stifle any cry of surprise. Gwen stiffened at the contact and her eyelids flew upward.

Deep blue orbs stared at him in a moment of panic. Focused at last, Gwen Philliphant recognized Eli

Holten. Her tensed body relaxed and tears filled her rounded eyes.

"Easy, Gwen. No need to cry. I came to tell you how we plan to free you. Can you sit up all right and listen?"

"Umm-uhnn," she muttered under his restraining hand.

Holten helped her upright. Immediately she flung her arms around his neck and pressed her cheek to his face.

"Oh, Eli, I . . . I feared I'd never see you again. I . . . thought we were going to be tortured and killed."

"Not much chance of that," Eli replied, likewise in a whisper. "Spotted Horse wants the railroad out, but no part of a war with the whites."

"We learned as much earlier. What do you expect to do to get us out?"

Quickly he explained the situation to her as he had done with her father. Gwen listened with mounting hope. She had not released her hold around the scout's neck and, when he finished his information, she tightened the grip while she kissed him fervently on the lips.

Her tongue began to probe and dart. She loosed one hand and slid it down his chest and belly to grasp at his ample manhood. This was hardly the time for passion, Eli considered. Then he flinched at how his traitorous body responded to her touch.

Against all reason and experience, his phallus stiffened rapidly in her grasp. Gwen began to slide her hand along its rising length, urging faster reaction. Gwen began to tremble and a soft moan escaped her. Her touch became insistent. In a fleeting moment, Eli tried to disengage himself. Then Gwen fumbled open the placket front of his trousers and freed his bulging organ.

"No, Gwen," he managed when their embrace

166

ended. "Not here and now. We haven't time. I have to get out of here without being detected."

"Oh, Eli, please. I . . . I can't bear it." She released him entirely and slumped down against his straining thighs. Her mouth quickly found the sensitive, fiery tip of his maleness and engulfed it with searing eagerness. Her tongue flicked tantalizing circles. Eli trembled and tried to pull away.

Gwen's head began to bob up and down, while one hand kneaded at the ample sack that hung below the root of his pulsing lance. The scout's belly tightened and a great shudder passed through him.

"Gwen, Gwen," he appealed. "I . . . I . . . oh, hell."

Resigned, and delighted in the surrender, Eli leaned back and gave the lovely young woman free reign on his bountiful member. She gulped eagerly, making small mewing sounds of pleasure, which he joined in his own abandon.

After a long, enervating five minutes, Gwen ceased and arranged herself on the buffalo robes, her skirt hiked high and her wetly gleaming cleft spread wide and welcoming. Eli could do nothing but oblige. Slowly he placed himself over her. She drew up her legs and lunged toward him as he directed his waving spear downward at its target.

Eli sank home in a splendrous explosion of delight. He began to work his hips, slowly at first, then with increasing power. Gwen rocked and moaned and clawed at his buckskin-covered back. Slowly, too slowly by the scout's reckoning, the sap began to rise. He plowed the lush field with deeper strokes until a wild crescendo took them over the brink into momentary oblivion.

"Oh, Eli. Oh, bless you. Now I know I'm alive."

Drained, the scout tidied himself and made ready to go. "And soon you'll be free. You're a wonder, Gwen.

But . . . there could have been better places and times for that. All the same, I love you for it. Sleep and get lots of rest. Be ready when someone gives you the word."

They kissed and Eli slipped from the lodge. He had passed the second ring of tipis, with safety only thirty yards away, when three Cheyenne warriors appeared in his path. The one in the middle he recognized at once as Spotted Horse.

"So this is how Tall Bear repays *Tsistsistas* hospitality and honors his truce?" the war leader demanded in a sarcastic tone.

"It's . . . not what you think, Spotted Horse."

"Isn't it? Did you come here to pick berries for your first-light meal?" He spoke rapidly in his own language to the two who accompanied him.

They stepped forward and disarmed the scout, then held him tightly at each side. Spotted Horse came closer. "You could be killed for this. Right here, now." The war chief paused and a fleeting flicker of smile crossed his lips. His eyes softened their flinty gaze.

"Yet, we danced for the eagle feather together. That makes us brothers. Why have you come, Tall Bear?"

Eli hung his head, feigning shame. "To see the white woman. She and I . . . we're . . ."

"The ways of the whites are soiled," Spotted Horse replied, scandalized by this admission. "You have lived too long among them. Our ways, and those of the Dakota, aren't like this. You're either a brave man or a fool. I think you not so foolish."

"What is this? What's going on?" Sterling Philliphant's voice sounded querulous as it grew closer through the thinning fog.

"This man. Have you seen him tonight?" Spotted Horse asked Philliphant in English.

Sterling Philliphant had achieved his success

through considerable shrewdness. He didn't need any time to evaluate the situation. His answer came quickly, a ring of sincerity in his words.

"No. No, I didn't. What *are* you doing here, Mister Holten?"

"I, uh, that is, er . . ." Eli replied, continuing his act, eyes cast downward.

Spotted Horse bought it. "He says he came to be with your daughter."

"You scoundrel!" Philliphant exploded. "You're reprehensible, sir."

"Do you wish us to kill him now?"

The proposal shocked the older man. He looked from the war chief to the scout in perplexity. Eli gave him a quick wink. Sterling Philliphant pursed his lips.

"Did you catch him coming or going?"

"I don't know."

Philliphant produced a frown. "Well then, no. No, I think not. Although I detest the thought of his compromising my daughter, I can't turn a fellow white man over to you to murder in cold blood. Mostly, Spotted Horse, because were I to do so, it would seriously hamper your efforts to stop my railroad without bloodshed and war. There must be some . . . other way?"

Spotted Horse considered it a moment. "Yes-s. There is another means to answer this insult. Tall Bear is a brave man. He knows our ways. He can be given a trial by combat. A chance to fight for his life and freedom. A warrior will be chosen to face him in a single battle. It will be a fight to the death. Are you agreed, Tall Bear?"

"I am."

"Now, just a minute," Philliphant protested.

"There can be no other way, Phil'pant," Spotted Horse snapped. "Isn't this better than simply finishing him without any chance?"

169

Grudgingly, the railroad magnate nodded agreement. "I suppose you're right. Do you really want to go through with this, Mister Holten?"

"I've already given my word. It'll be a fair fight, I can assure you of that."

"But, the odds, man."

"It's my life, after all. And it might be the only chance to keep these talks on a peaceful basis. Only one platoon came on this patrol. You know what's waiting at the rail-head. Without a peaceful solution, there'll be a bloodbath."

Sterling Philliphant considered the remainder of one company, and the other of cavalry and the small cannon encamped at the rail's end. What bitter irony, if his desire to do something to benefit the Indians ended in a terrible war. Eli Holten was right. No matter the outcome, this drama would have to be played out.

"Very well. It's your decision. When will this fight be, Spotted Horse?"

"When the sun is high. No talk tomorrow. Holten fight then."

Moving with exaggerated caution through the tall, damp buffalo grass, Corporal Michael Delaney made his way back to the lip of the creek bank. He lowered himself over the edge and started off at a trot. In excellent condition for a cavalryman, he didn't even pant when he reported to Lt. Harris.

"Sir, Corporal Delaney reporting, sir. Mister Holten has been discovered in the hostile camp, sir. He's been taken prisoner."

"What's this?" Gordon Harris demanded, rousing from a light nap.

"Yes, sir. From what I overheard, he's to fight to the death against some picked warrior tomorrow at noon."

"Corporal, pick your best man and send him off now to Captain Roberts. Request in my name that he dispatch the entire force forward. It's gonna be war now, Corporal."

"Yes, sir. If you say so. Only . . ."

"Do it at once, Corporal."

"Yes, sir."

After returning Delaney's salute, Gordon Harris strode about the small night camp with his hands clasped behind his back. Glorious. Yes, it would be his first taste of combat. He could hardly wait until the others arrived.

Throughout the night, visions of the awesome spectacle of a cavalry charge filled his head.

Chapter 19

Among men so given to exercising their jaws, the many Irish workmen at the PR&PR railhead maintained an unusual and uneasy silence at the morning meal. Meadow larks sang from close and far. Mother quail whistled instructions to their young, now nearly ready to leave the covey for life on their own. Only a few angry mutters rose from some of the narrow, fold-up tables. Men who had been close friends the previous evening eyed each other suspiciously across the kitchen car. Bursting with the terrible news he possessed, and frightened for having it, Timmy Pruett reported in sick and remained in his bunk. After breakfast, Archie Boyne found him there.

"What's the matter, Timmy?" the sandy-haired lad inquired.

"Oh, nothin', Archie."

"There has to be somethin' or ye wouldn't be layin there all pale and tremblin'. Come now, what is it?"

"It's . . . I can't tell you. It's too awful."

"Ye've come this far, Timmy. You know you can trust me. What is it?"

"H-how do you feel about unions?" Timmy blurted scared even the more for asking it. If only Sean were here, he thought miserably.

Archie shrugged. "I don't think about them one way

or the other. Me uncle says that the toffs who run things won't want them. That they're nothin' but a' invitation to jail. Me, I don't care. Why?"

"Th-there's gonna be union trouble right here. Today, I mean."

"Naw. How can that be?"

"It's true. I . . . I heard all about it last night." Once started, the entire story poured out. "Those three men came in with you. They're the ones leadin' it. An' the five fellers got here yesterday," he concluded. "They want to call a strike."

Archie threw up one hand in a Gaelic gesture. "What utter nonsense."

"It's *true*, Archie!" Tears formed in Timmy's eyes. "An' they talked like anyone who got in their way, they'd kill 'em."

"Are ye . . . are ye thinkin' that's maybe what happened to yer friend, Sean?"

"No. That was Injuns, plain and sure. Only, what can I do? I tried to see Mister Llewellyn last night. He laughed at me and said it was makin' a mountain outta a mole hill. Nobody will listen."

"I did. I'm sure me Uncle Brian will. Maybe he can convince the chief engineer."

"What if the ones plannin' this find out? They'll wring my neck and toss me under the ballast. No one will ever know what happened."

"Yer imaginin' too much, Timmy. Sure an' Uncle Brian'll watch out for ye. I'll go tell him right now."

"Please don't, Archie."

"Naw, naw, Timmy. Yer a good friend an' all. So's there's nothin' but to make this known to the right people an' see yer looked after all safe an' sound. I'll even take a gun and guard ye if yer so sure of the danger. Now, I'm for seein' Uncle Brian."

Lead wrapped around his heart, Timmy Pruett felt

as though he would sink through the floor of the dormitory car when his friend departed. How would Archie keep that man, Lavin, from finding out? He'd never live through that, Timmy knew.

Flogging a winded horse, the messenger from Lt. Harris arrived at the railhead shortly before noon. He saw an unusual number of men standing about idle, hands in pockets. Not his business, he shrugged it away and reported to Captain Roberts.

When Dave Roberts heard the news from the patrol, he summoned Winfield Stone and the company first sergeants. His mouth had thinned to a grim slash when the three came to him. At once he outlined the situation.

"We have only one choice in the circumstances. Let's assume that Eli loses this fight. Spotted Horse isn't likely to let Gordon Harris off lightly. He'll interpret the defeat as proof of dishonest intentions on the part of the Army. Once he engages Harris in a killing battle, it's war for sure. I want both companies fully equipped, mounted and ready to ride within half an hour."

"What about this labor trouble, Dave?" Winfield Stone asked.

"Not our concern. That's a civil matter. An Indian war is what we want to prevent. We'll leave a few men in camp to serve as messengers. The rest will ride out and let the railroaders solve their own problems."

"Yes, sir. First Sergeant," Stone responded, walking away while instructing his lead NCO on what he expected.

Behind them, Dave Roberts looked at the small six-pound galloper. Not an impressive cannon, by itself. To the Cheyenne, though, it would be devastating. And a

174

damned shame, too. How the hell did Eli get caught up in such a mess? Well, he had a job to do and he'd try to do it. Whatever the case, they'd arrive too damned late to help Eli. Holten would have to look out for himself.

"There go the so'jer boys, devil take 'em," Liam Daley growled.

"Right ye are. Time for us to get things stirred up, eh?"

"The sooner the better." Liam climbed onto a flatcar and raised his hands above his head. He spoke loudly and projected his voice, so that all for some distance could hear his words.

"You men. Those of you who have taken up your tools. Lay them down. The Army's ridden off, leavin' us exposed and unprotected again. Why is it? To rescue one of their own. *One man.* That shows how important we are to them. An' does this fine railroad do anything to stop them? *It does not!*

"Well, we're not waitin' for someone to protect us any more. Already there's the core of a union formed at this railhead. The International Collective of Railroad Workers, it is. There's men all among you who's newly made members. We're callin' on all of you to join us. Lay aside your tools and stand resolute against this murderous policy. Band together behind our call for a general strike until such time as our lives and our rights are safe from greed and indifference!"

"Yeah! That's right, you tell 'em, Liam," a voice called out from close to the flatcar.

"What er we gonna do if they just fire us all?" a dissenter inquired.

"They can't. There's no one else to build their damned railroad."

"What about those Chinamen you was talkin' about,

Liam?" another workman demanded.

"They ain't here now an' they can't get here if we tear up enough track behind us," Daley adroitly misdirected.

"We're with ya, Liam," a half dozen agitators exclaimed ringingly.

"Me, too!" a ballastman announced.

"Not I. I say we keep faith with the railroad," a burly gandy dancer objected.

A ragged cheer rose in his support, to be cut off abruptly when a meaty smack in the back of the head from a cudgel cut off the belligerent workman in midsentence.

"Oh, shit!" Timmy Pruett exclaimed aloud as he watched the gathering discontent from the narrow window of his dormitory car. It's happening too soon, his troubled thoughts continued. Now nothin' can be done to stop it.

Standing silently in a half-circle, the warriors of Spotted Horse waited for the trial by combat to begin. Sterling Philliphant stood beside the war leader, a grim expression clouding his face. Despite his objections, his daughter had also come to the mid-day ordeal. A moment passed and the two braves who had guarded Eli Holten through the night brought the scout to the designated place. At a nod from Spotted Horse, Eats-His-Horse stepped forward.

"Choose your weapon," he said simply.

"I'd prefer to use my Remington," Eli answered lightly. "That being out, I'll settle for a tomahawk."

"Hunh! A good choice. You are brave, Tall Bear."

"I've no doubt you are too. Shall we get on with it?"

Eats-His-Horse nodded and went to obtain their weapons. Philliphant turned to Spotted Horse.

"Isn't there some way to prevent this? Killing Holten can only undo all the good we've accomplished so far."

"This is a personal fight. Tall Bear knows that it has nothing to do with the soldiers of your iron road. He has to redeem his honor."

"My God!" the railroad president exclaimed. "Has everyone gone mad but me?"

Grunts of satisfaction and anticipation came from the gathered warriors as Eats-His-Horse returned with two well-balanced tomahawks. One he handed to an apprentice warrior, who took it to Eli Holten.

"Thank you, boy," Eli told the little lad.

"Begin." Spotted Horse declared.

Holten and his opponent started a shuffling movement, circling each other. They crouched, their steel-bladed 'hawks extended to nearly arm's length. The deadly hatchets weaved slightly as the contestants sized up each other. Gradually, the distance between them closed. Suddenly Eats-His-Horse leaped forward and struck with his weapon.

With the agility of a mountain sheep, the scout jumped backward. Metal rang loudly as he parried the overhand blow. A thoughtful expression flitted over the Cheyenne warrior's face. He tried to close again.

Holten flicked out with his killing axe and a shout went up from the spectators. A thin, red line appeared on Eats-His-Horse's right forearm. It opened swiftly and blood began to run. His eyes registered his surprise.

A shallow cut, he realized. Yet, the white Oglala had drawn first blood. Eats-His-Horse rolled his shoulders and shifted direction, moving crab-wise to his left. To his amazement, Holten countered and began to close. The distance narrowed. Eats-His-Horse swung his 'hawk in a horizontal arc, the keen edge swishing past only an inch from the scout's exposed belly.

Eli took a forward step and smashed the heavy spiked end of the 'hawk into Eats-His-Horse's shoulder. The Cheyenne grunted and danced sideways. His weapon fell from nerveless fingers. Blood streamed down his right side. He bent quickly, to avoid another pass and scooped up a handful of pebbles.

These he hurled at the scout's face. Then he dashed forward and retrieved his tomahawk in a left hand grip. Instantly, he slashed upward at Holten's belly. Eli held his ground, though, and slammed the flat of his blade into the side of his opponent's head.

Rubber-legged, Eats-His-Horse wobbled two faltering paces and went to his knees. Lips compressed, Holten moved in for the final stroke.

From some hidden resource, Eats-His-Horse rallied. He whipped his tomahawk around in a short curve. The sharp edge bit into buckskin and nicked flesh below. Pain raced up Eli's leg. He stumbled, then had to leap desperately away to avoid the backhand stroke that would have emasculated him had it struck. Shouts of encouragement rose among the Cheyenne warriors. Gwen Philliphant cried out in horror and covered her eyes. Holten scuffed dust into his attacker's eyes with his moccasin-clad left foot and danced away.

Blood ran down his right leg, soaking his moccasin. Eli concentrated on his tricky opposition. The hell of it was he didn't want to kill Eats-His-Horse. But it began to look like he'd have to. While his mental debate progressed, the Cheyenne warrior came to his feet, wiping away the dirt that had stung his eyes. In a wild rush, he came after the scout.

Sweat rolled over Eli's body. He ached in every joint and a faint dizziness made him unsteady on his feet. Eats-His-Horse's tomahawk became a flashing blur before the scout's face. Once more he had to retreat. Weakness washed over Eli, reminding him of his recent

178

bout with pneumonia. He'd have to end this fast or go down with that blade sunk in him somewhere. Relentlessly, his opponent moved in.

"Now!" a brave shouted.

"Finish him!" another cried.

"Kill the *nia'tha!*"

Holten bobbed and shuffled to his left, relying on his strong leg. Eats-His-Horse came after him again. Salty beads of moisture rolled into the scout's eyes. He blinked furiously to rid himself of the stinging intrusion. The air moaned close to his ear and instinct sent him forward, so that the haft, rather than the blade of the 'hawk slammed into his shoulder. Fiery agony erupted from the abused spot. Holten rammed the handle of his weapon into the yielding flesh of Eats-His-Horse's belly.

Air whooshed out of the brawny warrior's lungs. He staggered backward and fought to replenish the missing oxygen. Eli rammed a knee sharply up into the Indian's groin. He felt the yielding flesh of penis and testicles at the same time Eats-His-Horse groaned and began to sag. Charged by a fresh jolt of adrenaline, Holten swung his tomahawk toward the head of the bent-over man.

The blade hit flat against the side of Eats-His-Horse's head with an ugly smacking sound. The warrior dropped face-first into the dirt, unconscious and bleeding from mangled flesh above his right ear. Eli Holten stepped back.

Slowly, the panting scout raised both arms above his head. *"Maka kin le, mitawa ca!"* he shouted triumphantly in Lakota.

Right then he felt like he *did* own the earth. The whole fight had taken less than two minutes. Staggering slightly, Eli walked to where Spotted Horse watched. He handed the war chief his tomahawk.

"You didn't slay him," Spotted Horse observed.

"No need to. He fought bravely. It would be a shame to deprive the *Tsistsistas* of a man with such courage."

A smile creased Spotted Horse's face. "You are truly a man of honor, Tall Bear. When Eats-His-Horse recovers he will feast you and then talk of the railroad." Spotted Horse smiled again, pleased with his easy use of the new word.

Chapter 20

Guard relief came shortly before dawn. As the two off-duty sentries strolled back to the camp from the railhead, a pink band began to spread on the eastern horizon. When their eyes adjusted to the increasing brightness, a grisly sight awaited them.

"Holy shit! Our asses are sure going to be in a crack for this," one soldier exclaimed.

His buddy stood in mute shock, staring at the mutilated corpses sprawled on the ground. Arrows bristled from the bodies, they had been scalped and disemboweled. Their entrails lay in gruesome coils around them. Bitter bile rose in the unspeaking trooper's throat and he bent forward, retching.

Despite his worry over possible disciplinary action, the first trooper raised his voice in an urgent hail. "Corporal of the guard! There's dead men near the railroad."

"How the hell could this have happened?" the astonished noncom demanded when he trotted to where the pair waited.

"I don't know, Corporal Myers. I'll swear they weren't there when we went on duty at two o'clock. We didn't see anything or hear anything."

Lieutenant Dahlgrin, a sergeant and three men from his platoon of C Company ran up. "What do you make of this, Corporal?"

"Hard to say right now, sir. The sentries swear there was no disturbance last night and they saw no one moving around." He knelt beside one of the dead men. "There's not a lot of blood around for . . . for what was done to them. It could be they were killed somewhere else and brought here."

Dahlgrin looked around. "Does that sound like Indians to any of you?"

"No, sir," Sergeant Poole answered immediately.

The others expressed agreement with this.

"Well then, what do we have here? Someone killed these men. If it wasn't the Cheyenne, who could it be? For the time being, I want you to keep any remarks or speculation about this strictly to yourselves. Don't mention it to anyone. Sergeant Poole, I want a messenger sent to Captain Roberts. Inform him of what has happened and our suspicions."

"Right away, sir." Poole saluted and trotted off.

"We'd better inform the railroad people. And get someone to cover these bodies," the lieutenant directed Myers.

The non-com's news met with immediate reaction. He found Brendon Llewellyn discussing the previous day's drop in production with Arthur Lavin. The chief engineer scowled and shook his head sadly. Lavin went red in the face and slammed a fist against the surface of his small desk.

"That really ties it. Another sneaky Indian attack, two men dead. There's no stopping the men now, Mister Llewellyn. There'll be a general strike for sure."

"Strike? But there's no union among the track crews," Llewellyn returned.

"Those men who slacked off yesterday afternoon are

182

talking about an outfit called the International Collective of Railroad Workers. I've a suspicion they've had an organizer or two among those newly hired." Lavin pointed through the open door of the office car. "The word's already getting around. Look at those ballastmen standing by the bodies."

"I'll put a stop to this strike talk damned fast," Llewellyn growled. "Can I count on you to help, Arthur?"

Lavin smiled thinly. "I'll do what I can."

An hour later, not a single man had reported for work. Those who would have done so refrained as a result of less-than-subtle intimidation. Among them were Brian O'Dwyer, Archie Boyne and Timmy Pruett. The man and two boys walked away from the knots of angry workmen. Alone, on the far side of the tracks, Brian spoke up.

"Sure an' I'm afraid ye were right, Timmy, lad. It's just like you said. A general strike it is. Lord help us, we'll all wind up without jobs. Two men murdered. Now I don't know a thing about Injuns, but it makes me wonder. Those boys were against the strike idea. Talked a lot among the others. Then they wind up dead this mornin'."

"They were killed with the same kind of arrows as Sean," Timmy replied. "The scalping and cuttin' them open like that are sure enough Indian ways. Only . . . I wonder if there's not more behind this?"

"Such as what?"

"That Arthur Lavin and the men he hangs around. He told them that anyone who made too much fuss over the strike would have to be taken care of."

"Could they have done for Sean, too?" Archie piped up.

Tears filled Timmy's eyes. "If . . . if they did . . . then that means, ah, that any of us could be killed and

183

the Indians blamed for it. Mister O'Dwyer, I can't help it, I'm scared."

To punctuate Timmy's declaration, a loud blast sounded from some distance down the tracks. Sections of rail flew into the air and a heavy cloud of dust and powder smoke obscured the scene.

Most of the earlier *bon homme* had returned to the Cheyenne camp by the morning following Eli Holten's single combat. He had purchased three sleek ponies from Spotted Horse and taken them to the lodge where Eats-His-Horse lay recovering from his injuries. The youthful Cheyenne warrior beamed at this generous gift and clasped forearms with the scout.

"You're a true Oglala, Tall Bear," Eats-His-Horse declared. "I'm proud to have fought against you. Now we will be friends?"

"Gladly, if that's what you wish," Eli replied.

"I'm hungry," the smiling brave complained. He ran fingers gingerly around a large, purplish bruise on his head. "And my head feels like I've been kicked by a horse. See if you can find us something to eat."

"Right away." Holten stepped out of the low lodge and summoned a boy of twelve or so. "Bring meat and salt for Eats-His-Horse and me," he requested in Lakota.

Grinning, the gangly youth ran to obey his orders. Eli smiled after him, then changed his expression to one of warm welcome when he saw Gwen Philliphant walking his direction.

"Good morning," he greeted her.

"Eli, you astonish me. Here yesterday you nearly died in a fight, now you look chipper as an Eastern beau come a-courting."

"I'd like to be courting you right now," Eli responded.

The rich baritone of his voice sent shivers of excitement through Gwen's graceful frame. She loved to hear Eli talk like that. Impulsively she stepped closer and laid a hand on his arm. She looked about in exasperation.

"If only there was . . . somewhere safe."

"All we need to do is ride a way along the creek," he suggested hopefully.

Gwen made a sour face. "Since you got caught the other night, Daddy's been watching me so closely I feel like a mouse with a hungry cat after me."

"What we need to do, then, is put a bell on the cat," Eli teased.

"I mean it," Gwen replied with an impatient stamp on her foot. "He's got marriage on his mind."

"Ummm, ah, Gwen, that's hardly what I am planning for."

"Nor I, truth to tell. Though . . . it would be wonderful, I think to . . . oh, never mind."

"Speaking of your father, here he comes."

"Ah, good morning, Mister Holten. I've been considering the situation. I wonder, given your reestablished respect with these warriors, isn't it a good time to open serious talks with Spotted Horse about ending his attacks on the railroad?"

For a moment Holten had thought the railroad owner was about to bring up the subject he had been discussing with Gwen. Compared to that, this topic seemed trivial. He cleared his throat.

"I'd like to talk with the cavalry patrol that accompanied me. We should send a message to Captain Roberts and have him come up for the talks. That is if it's all right with you."

"Certainly. The more impressive we can make our presentation, the more likely to get a favorable agreement. Will Spotted Horse let you ride out of camp?"

185

"I don't see why not. He had agreed to a meeting before. Nothing should be changed now. Let's go see him."

Spotted Horse greeted the two white men warmly. Of course, he would be willing to talk about the railroad. Holten could go and get his soldier friends. He concluded with a hearty slap on the scout's left shoulder.

"We make a big feast tonight. You and Eats-His-Horse dance your fight for us and soldiers. That be a good thing. Go now. Come back soon."

Eli rode Sonny out to where Lt. Harris waited. The young officer had a drawn look and his eyes widened with surprise and relief when the scout approached.

"Jesus, Eli, I can't believe you're still alive. I watched that fight with field glasses. More than once I figured you to be a goner."

"I managed," Holten allowed modestly. "Spotted Horse is ready to talk. He says to ride in any time this afternoon. There'll be a big feast and tall tale telling tonight, then the serious discussion gets under way. I'd like to have Davey Roberts here by tomorrow some time."

"He should be here before that," Harris informed the scout. "I sent a messenger off when Corporal Delaney came back with the story about you being taken captive."

"Hummm," Eli returned in frowning contemplation. "I hope he don't come all set for war."

"After what I sent about the fight you were to have, that's likely to be how it is."

"Damn. Well, I'd better get back and prepare Spotted Horse for a show of force. Davey's level-headed enough when it comes to dealing with Indians. So long as he doesn't come in here shooting it should work out."

"I, ah, told him that in my estimation the situation

186

warranted bringing along the, ah, cannon."

"Awh shit!" the scout groaned.

Captain David Roberts rode at the head of the long column of cavalry. He had pushed the men through the night. They had walked more than they rode, cautious not to injure the horses. All the same they covered miles. Dave cursed the slowness of travel. He didn't know what he would find. Eli Holten alive or dead? The prairie ablaze with a new Indian campaign? God, don't make this another Custer fiasco, he prayed.

"Sir? Captain Roberts," one of the messengers who had ridden to the railhead interrupted his troubled thoughts.

"Yes, what is it?"

"From the looks of the ground around here, sir, we can't be more'n an hour or so from where Lieutenant Harris and the platoon waited for Mister Holten."

"We've made better time than I thought," Dave responded thoughtfully.

A smooth-faced corporal galloped his mount forward from the tail of the column to report to the commander. "Dispatch rider from the railhead, sir," he called out as he reined in and saluted.

"What now?" Dave griped, certain it boded no good for his mission.

He learned soon enough, when the trooper arrived.

"Two railroad workers killed night before last, sir. It looks like the Cheyenne did it. Only Lieutenant Dahlgrin doesn't think so." At Roberts' bidding, he explained the situation in detail.

"There's not a damn thing we can do about it," Dave Roberts told Winfield Stone. "We're out in the middle of nowhere and no real jurisdiction over that sort of crime anyway. The only thing to do is push on and find out what the situation is with the Cheyenne."

Seated in Spotted Horse's lodge, Eli Holten, Lt.
Gordon Harris and Sterling Philliphant had finished
the noon meal when a shrill yip outside attracted their
attention. A warrior thrust his head inside the lodge.

"Many soldiers come," he rattled off in Cheyenne.

Spotted Horse frowned slightly. "How many?"

"Nearly a number to equal our own."

The Cheyenne war leader came to his feet and led
the way out of the tipi. Some five hundred yards away a
long blue line filled the western horizon. With the
exception of a couple of squads, Eli Holten judged, two
entire companies of cavalry waited in formation to
charge. Near the center of the troops, sunlight twinkled merrily off the highly-polished brass tube of a six
pound galloper. Shot and shell to rain deadly havoc
among the Cheyenne. Involuntarily, Holten winced.

"Is this how Tall Bear and the iron horse man talk
peace?" Spotted Horse demanded, suddenly angry.

Holten swallowed and faced the furious Cheyenne
"The war leader of these soldiers is a close friend o
mine. Lieutenant Harris here sent a message about my
fight with Eats-His-Horse. Without knowledge of wha
happened, they sent too many. It's not a threat to you
Spotted Horse. Let me ride out and explain."

Spotted Horse nodded. "I will come with you. Also
Bear Heart and Owl Friend."

Clever, Holten thought. Not about to let me g
alone. He smiled and nodded approval. Spotted Horse
called for ponies, his lance and shield. Mounted, th
small party rode forward. Tommy Red Hawk spotte
Eli Holten and pointed him out to Dave Roberts.

"Eli's with 'em, Cap'n."

"I see him, Tommy. Let's meet them half way an

find out what's going on."

Tension built to a nearly intolerable level as the officer and scout detached themselves from the line of soldiers and walked their horses toward the approaching group from the camp. Silence filled the ranks, and held the Cheyenne warriors in check. The parties met in a small grassy depression.

"You made good time, Davey," Eli said easily.

"I gather everything is all right with yo... came the captain's reply. "Harris seems to have ... reacted a little in recommending the cannon."

"That he did. Spotted Horse isn't too happy about that. He, ah, speaks English by the way."

"I see." Dave gave a "well then" shrug and addressed the Cheyenne war chief. "Spotted Horse, you and your warriors have been attacking the railroad. Why is that?"

"We don't want it to cross this land and that to the west. Game is scared away by the iron horse. If we can't hunt, we cannot eat."

"That's a straight-forward enough answer," Dave looked to Eli for some indication of what to say next. The scout nodded toward the encampment. "I'm sure there's a better place to discuss this."

Spotted Horse produced a knowing smile. "We were to feast this night and talk. As soldier chief, you would come to this council?"

"My pleasure. Let me get my troops accommodated and I'll join you within the hour."

"You will be welcome."

A pipe was smoked and some wrangling, preliminary speeches made by members of Spotted Horse's council before Dave and Eli managed to get away alone to discuss what all had happened. Eli went first, explaining about his single combat, omitting that the cause of his discovery had been a stolen tryst with

189

Gwen Philliphant. Then Dave sprang the news of the recent killings on his friend.

"Davey, it couldn't have been the Cheyenne. Not a warrior has left this camp in four days."

"Dahlgrin seems to think there's some foul play back at the railroad. Something about it being Cheyenne didn't ring true. He didn't send a detailed report, but I gathered he has another answer he's working on. The hell of it is, we don't have the authority to do anything about it."

"True enough," Eli agreed.

"In which case, what can we possibly do to keep the peace and find out who is responsible?"

"That we might find out tonight at the feast," the scout suggested with a droll smile.

Chapter 21

Spotted Horse sat with his chin on one fist, contemplating what he had just been told. Two railroad men killed. Arrows marked like those of the Cheyenne. It couldn't be. For him, the feast had lost its savor.

"None of my warriors have been raiding since we take Phil'pant and the woman."

"Far as I can tell, no one has left camp," Eli repeated from his earlier remark.

"The soldiers will look for who did this?"

"The Army can do nothing. There's no reason to doubt that someone else is responsible," Eli told Spotted Horse. "So the Army has no power to investigate."

"If *Tsistsistas* did this, the soldiers would come after us?"

"That's correct."

A sardonic smile shaped on Spotted Horse's broad face. "Then it's for the white man's law to punish who did this," he declared.

"That would be difficult," Dave Roberts informed him. "The nearest white lawmen are too far away to risk the time we'd lose going for them and bringing them back. Those responsible could be long gone by then. There is a strike among the railroad workers."

"What is 'strike'?"

"The men have quit working, Spotted Horse. They

191

say it's not safe." Dave Roberts couldn't resist adding a small jibe. "In part, you're responsible for this."

"Good. No work, no iron road." He frowned then, the full import of their argument becoming obvious. "But, if we get blame for killing men, soldiers could make war?"

"That depends on who tells the story and what they say," Eli answered smoothly. "Whoever is responsible is a danger to you every bit as much as to us. Mister Philliphant has nearly two hundred workers at the end of the track. They are on strike, fighting the railroad. If they manage to arm themselves, the situation could become rather ugly. Particularly if those who organized this strike had something to do with the murders. As we've said before, the Army can do nothing in civilian affairs such as this. Certain others aren't bound by the same restrictions."

A fleeting smile curled the corners of Spotted Horse's mouth as he asked with mock innocence, "Who would that be?"

"The Cheyenne for instance," Eli replied with a straight face.

Spotted Horse threw back his head and laughed heartily. His eyes twinkled and he shook with the peals of his merriment. When he recovered his composure, he slapped Holten on one shoulder.

"Ho! Tall Bear. I like this. You and I would be fighting on the same side? How could this be done?"

The biggest obstacle had been overcome, Holten acknowledged with an inward sigh of relief. "What we'd need is a little diversion. Some excuse for the Army to get involved in the matter of the strike and these murders. Say, an attack by your warriors?"

Humor bubbled up in the war leader once more. "Why have I not thought of this before? Who would believe it? The Red Paint People and the soldiers

192

fighting together against an enemy." Spotted Horse crowed. Then he sobered. "What of the iron road? After this is over, what then?"

"I've already told you how I believe my railroad will help your people, rather than harm them." Sterling Philliphant leaned toward his host in a gesture of earnestness. "You've said there are few Cheyenne left in this part of the country. That most have been sent south. Yet, you predict that the others will come back."

"This is so."

"If they do, then you'll need every source of supply. There's something I've been thinking about that I want to add. The railroad will pay your people for the use of the land. We can do that in the form of goods and free freight charges, or in money."

Spotted Horse thought a moment. "What about in guns and bullets?"

"No chance of that, my friend. Only think of what I've offered. We can talk of it again when the troubles are ended at the railhead. Will you agree to that?"

Slowly, Spotted Horse nodded.

"Here's how I figure it should be done," Eli Holten injected. "I'll leave with a small party, well ahead of the rest. I want to look around the troubles at the track first. Spotted Horse, you and your warriors will make another attack on my signal." Carefully, Eli laid out the rest of his plan.

When he concluded, Capt. Dave Roberts spoke crisply. "Lieutenant Stone, have the men alerted to be ready to move out at first light. We're returning to the railhead. Our, ah, Cheyenne auxiliaries will depart ahead of us."

"Damn it all," Brendon Llewellyn exploded in frustration. "We might as well be out-and-out prisoners.

193

Locked up here in Sterling's private car, we can't even call for help from the Army."

Gathered around him were the railroad personnel not engaged in the general strike. Present were Regis, of course, Philliphant's personal cook, Isaac Bingham, the paymaster clerk, the five man survey crew, the engineer and fireman of the work train. Also confined with them were Brian O'Dwyer, Archie Boyne and Timmy Pruett. Mike Malloy and the other foremen had been added to the list of non-strikers. Outside, the workers stood about idle.

Once in a while one or two would rouse themselves to shout imprecations at the "lackeys of management," confined in the president's car. Their leaders had broken into the armory in the express car and the men were heavily armed. This, too, gave cause for grave concern to the chief construction engineer and foremen.

"They blew up track down the line yesterday," Llewellyn went on, enumerating the damage done by the strikers. "What can we expect next?"

"Nothin' good, from what young Timmy's been tellin' me," Brian O'Dwyer injected.

Llewellyn turned to the burly track man and his youthful charges. His face became serious as he stepped close to Timmy, a hand outstretched.

"Son, I owe you an apology. I'm sorry now I didn't listen to you the other night. Did they really say that anyone not in support of the strike would be 'gotten rid of?"

"Yes, sir," Timmy piped in his high, thin voice. He accepted the engineer's handshake. Pride at being taken seriously, at being treated like a man swelled his small chest.

"Then, could it be that . . . those men who were killed . . . ?"

"Damned right it might not o' been Injuns, Mister Llewellyn," Mike Malloy declared. "Includin', I'll wager, Sean O'Casey." He scowled darkly. "Sean was a dear friend o' mine. If I learn it were any o' that ICRW bunch done him in, I'll bust heads from here to New York."

"*If* yez get out of here alive, ye mean," Patrick McCrae added darkly.

A loud blast came from outside, as though to underscore McCrae's grim prediction. Close enough for the shock wave to rock the car, it sent the men inside to the windows on the right side.

"Christ! They've blown the water tower," Brendon Llewellyn exclaimed. "The Cheyenne couldn't burn it down but those sons of bitches destroyed it in seconds with a few sticks of dynamite. They've gone crazy."

"Th-think they might try it with this car?" Archie asked fearfully.

"Oh, hell, they . . . could get worked up enough, I suppose," Marvin Ross, the chief surveyor acknowledged reluctantly.

"What can we do?" Regis inquired, his eyes showing large portions of white.

"We can fight our way out of here," Mike Malloy declared strongly. "They come and check on us from time to time, right? So, when they do, we jump 'em, take their rifles and shoot our way to the Army camp."

"Hummm," Brian speculated. "It might work. Sure n' it'd be a better chance if we had some guns to start with. Once the soldiers see what's happening, they'll give us cover fire, ye can be sure o' that."

"Some of us might get killed," one of the more timid surveyors protested.

"*All* of us might if we stay here," Malloy countered. "Are we agreed, then? We'll make a break for the soldiers?"

195

Agreement went the rounds. In the silence that followed, Brendon Llewellyn injected a new thought.

"Regis, doesn't Sterling keep some firearms in here?"

"Yas, sah. Some sportin' arms. A brace of shotguns, a long range rifle."

"That takes care of three of us. Break them out, man. And all the ammunition you can find."

"By all the saints," Brian exclaimed. "They're bound to come say something about the water tower. We can be out of here in no time."

Frigid blasts of wind had come down out of the northeast. Dense cloud cover quickly formed, piling high, into thunderheads that threatened a heavy downpour. Eli Holten and his small detail raced along ahead of the impending storm, hopeful of finding shelter before it struck. Behind him rode the Cheyenne and a bit beyond them the cavalry. There couldn't be a worse time, he conceded, for a change in the weather.

Freezing rain began to fall an hour before sundown. The scout led his group into the shelter of a stand of willows near the ford of a creek. The frozen droplets made a constant rattle on the slender, yellowing leaves.

"Get a fire going." Eli directed as he stripped the saddle and blanket off Sonny. "We'll rest and eat something. When this passes over, we'll go on. Force march all night. I want to be at the railhead early as possible tomorrow."

Corporal Delaney wiped a wrist over his brow. "We could be in for another blizzard."

"Not likely. Whatever we get will be nasty enough. It should dampen spirits among the strikers, though. Give us a chance to learn more before the rest arrive."

Coffee, beans and other staples of the trail began to appear. The heady aroma of roasted and ground

196

Arbuckle's came from the inner triple-layer bag when Delaney opened the tin container. The three other men, finished now with gathering wood, tended to their mounts.

"Get that to brewing, Delaney," Holten urged. "You could save me from eternal torment with a cup of coffee right now."

"Ye save easy, Mister Holten."

"That we'll see when we reach the railroad."

Over their simple meal, Holten and Delaney discussed what waited for them at the end of their ride.

"I'll go in among the strikers," the scout planned aloud. "Uniforms might make them too edgy. You and the others learn what you can from the detachment left behind. Make a complete report and ride back to inform Captain Roberts of the situation."

"An' what about yerself?"

"I'll stay among them until after the Cheyenne 'attack.' Then, when the troops ride in, we'll make short work of the strike leaders. Once they're arrested, we can look into the murders."

Delaney smiled grimly. "It's gonna come as a shock to whoever did those fellers in to learn that the Cheyenne had been under close observation. They'll have a hard time convincin' anyone of their story then."

"That's what we're counting on, Delaney."

After the meal, Holten suggested the men try to get a little sleep. It took no urging to get the troopers to comply. Eli likewise dropped off in a light doze.

About nine that night the storm blew away to the southwest. The scout rose immediately and began to saddle his Morgan stallion. Within fifteen minutes the detail had made ready to move on.

"Long way to go," Holten reminded them. "The ground can be treacherous after an ice storm. We'll head off walking our mounts. Saddle up soon as we're clear."

"Blasted damn weather," Liam Daley growled as he huddled around a fitfully whipping fire near the ruins of the water tower.

"Freezin' rain. Just the thing for it, boys," an unaccountably cheerful gandy dancer mocked from a short distance off.

"That bunch we're keepin' from the others has got it lucky," Devon Flynn observed. "Sittin' nice and comfortable in that private car, not a worry in the world, while we stand out here and turn to ice."

"We've got the office and the express car," Percy Throckmorton lisped.

"You mean, Arthur's got them," Daley snarled. "While we freeze."

"Fok this cold weather," Rincón exploded. "The *pinché puto* here could go blow those *cabrónes* out of the private car with some of his dynamite, no?"

"An' wreck it so's it wouldn't be any good for us, either," Flynn complained. Naw. We oughtta go over there and drag 'em out by their scruffy necks and kick their butts a way back along the tracks toward Omaha."

Several of the uncomfortable strikers exchanged looks. Liam Daley nodded as though reaching a conclusion.

"Let's do just that," the labor organizer announced.

Led by Daley, half a dozen men started toward the private car.

"They're comin'," Timmy Pruett called out from the darkened interior of a sleeping compartment. "Liam Daley and five others."

"Make ready," Mike Malloy hissed.

A few moments later, the rear door banged open and Liam Daley stomped in, with two husky gandy dancers shouldering their way behind. "All right, off yer lazy asses and get outta this car. Yer gonna take a little hike to Omaha."

Daley started to say more, only to snap his mouth closed when he saw he faced the twin barrels of a ten gauge Parker shotgun.

"Keep yer mouth shut," Mike Malloy whispered harshly. "Don't try to give any alarm. Step inside and hand us yer guns." When the trio obeyed, Mike gave his next instruction. "Now, call the others."

"Would ye look at that," Corporal Delaney exclaimed as he pointed ahead.

The small group with Eli Holten had topped a long prairie swell and gazed down on the railroad track. The first thing they saw was the blasted water tower. Clumps of men stood around here and there and a number gestured angrily toward the army tents removed from the work train by some seventy-five yards.

"There's been some dirty work going on," Eli remarked, eyes picking out other signs. "Look back along the track. Someone blew up a couple of sections."

"Those boys are ridin' high, all right."

"We'd better split up here, Delaney. It don't look like Army blue is the favorite color with those workmen right now."

"It's the damn' Army's fault," Luke Partridge complained to Arthur Lavin as the scout cantered up five minutes later.

"No. Delaney brought it on himself. If he'd left them where they were, this couldn't have happened. He's just damned lucky they didn't take him prisoner."

"Howdy," the scout said non-committally. "What did Daley bring on himself, if I may ask?"

Arthur Lavin looked up angrily. "It's a long story.

199

You're with the soldier-boys," he accused. "Why aren't you over at their camp?"

"I'm a civilian, remember? I got away from the Cheyenne and came back here. Unless Captain Roberts is there, I've got no one to report to."

Lavin considered Holten's explanation. "Bein' a civilian, how do you take to strikes?"

"They can be mighty damned inconvenient. Though sometimes they are no doubt necessary. Why do you ask?"

"Because there's a general strike called here. You'd best be picking sides. Us or the management."

Eli looked around him at the armed, determined men, who now closed in from all sides. He shrugged and forced a strained smile. Then he wet his lips and canted his head to one side.

"I suppose I should put in my lot with the civilian brothers," he said, dismounting. "You know, I've often thought that contract scouts should have a union. Then maybe we wouldn't have to take so many risks. How about some grub? After that you can tell me what I need to know about this strike."

Chapter 22

Far out on the prairie, the wild creatures slowly began to recover from the effects of the sudden sleet storm. Prairie dogs peeped from their burrows. Snakes lost their sluggishness and moved with more vitality. A meadowlark began a tentative trill. A buffalo calf bleated hungrily for its mother. Hawks took to the wing, in search of slow-paced prey. Amid the reawakening, Capt. David Roberts and the troopers of his command pressed onward with all possible speed.

"Dave, we've still a hell of a way to go," Winfield Stone observed. He had ridden forward at his superior's request to discuss the upcoming confrontation with the striking railroaders.

"True. We don't want to get there ahead of time. My bet is the Cheyenne laid over even longer than we did. Indians can get mighty lazy when it comes to sudden, unexpected changes in the weather. The idea is for them to get there first. We're riding in to 'rescue' the workers. In the process we isolate those responsible for the strike and put an end to it. Of course we're doing that in order to better organize to fight the 'Cheyenne threat.' "

Stone slapped a gauntleted hand on his thigh. "I

swear, you and Eli Holten can cook up some of the craziest schemes. This is just barely on the edge of legality."

"Problem is for someone to figure out on which edge." Captain Roberts gave C Company's commander a wink.

The lieutenant's face went blank with astonishment. "You mean . . . ? What we're doin' isn't exactly by the book?"

Dave grinned. "Outside of Saturday morning inspections, when has anything we've done out here gone by the book? Exactly or any other way?"

Stone shook his head. "I can remember Eli sayin', 'If it gets the job done, do it.' I never thought it through before is all. So, if any of those labor fellows are of a mind to, they could file a complaint."

"If they're in any position to do so afterward. There's still those murders to account for." Dave Roberts looked up and signaled for a halt when he recognized Tommy Red Hawk cantering toward them.

"How far to go?" he greeted the scout.

"Two, three hours. The *Sahiela* are a mile ahead of us."

"Good. This should work out right the way Eli wants it."

Eli Holten circulated among the striking workers. Arthur Lavin remained at his side, answering questions, shading his remarks to put the walk-out in a good light. At last they reached the express car. So far everything had seemed orderly. No overt signs of violence like that which had obviously been done over the past several days. At Lavin's invitation, Eli entered the thick-walled strong room.

The first thing the scout noticed was that all the

arms racks had been emptied. Three men sat around the unused pot-belly stove. One chewed on a stump of cigar while the other two played a desultory game of stud poker. Lavin made the introductions.

"These are the officers of the ICRW chapter here at the railhead. Liam Daley, Devon Flynn and Luke Partridge. This is Eli Holten, a *civilian* scout for the Army. He's interested in learning more about labor organizations." A slight tone of mockery had entered Lavin's voice, the scout noted.

"Are you alone in this, Holten?" the shifty-eyed, red-faced man introduced as Liam Daley inquired.

"I am for the time being. I know a considerable number of other scouts who have complained about our, uh, work conditions," he invented as he kept track of subtle shifts in attitude and attention. "How difficult would it be to organize a union for people employed by the government?"

Luke Partridge grunted explosively, riffling his red beard. "Damn' near impossible. The gover'ment's in league with the plutocrats to keep the working man ground down in his, ah, proper place."

"Frontier scouts are noted more for their strong sense of individualism," Arthur Lavin bored in, "rather than responsibility of group consciousness that binds workers together back East. Isn't that so?"

"Well, we are a great deal freer out here," Holten evaded, wondering how close the Cheyenne and two companies of the 12th had come so far. "There's more room for a man to move about. To change his job if the conditions don't suit him."

"Yet, you say that's not the case for contract scouts?"

"The Army can get mighty bossy at times."

Their conversation went on in that vein for half an hour. The questions directed at the scout became more pointed. Lacking any more fabrications, and concerned that those he had glibly put out might trip him, Eli decided to be more direct himself.

"One thing that bothers me, and the other two scouts with this expedition, is the death of those three workmen. We're faced with that sort of danger all the time and no one seems to care any more about our safety than those poor fellers."

"*We* care, I can assure you of that," Lavin responded.

"What I wonder most is, how did they really die?"

A ripple of suppressed emotion ran through the four men around Eli Holten. The scout noticed it and kept his face blank of any betraying expression. Partridge and Lavin exchanged a long, brooding glance.

"Why, the stinkin' Cheyenne did them in," Devon Flynn blurted into the ominous silence that held in the express car.

"I'm . . . not so sure of that," Eli drawled his answer.

"What do you mean by that?" Luke Partridge demanded.

"A few days ago, when the last two were killed, none of the Cheyenne were out on a raid. They were all in camp, watching a single combat between a warrior named Eats-His-Horse and me. Which means that someone else did those fellers in. Since you gentlemen are concerned about it, I thought you ought to know that there might be a murderer on the loose among you."

Another significant glance passed between Partridge and Lavin. "You said you were in this alone?" Partridge queried.

"That's right."

The quartet of labor organizers relaxed a bit. "In that case, I think you should know that the men who were killed opposed the formation of an ICRW chapter and the strike."

"Does that include Sean O'Casey?" Holten asked in

an offhand manner.

"Yes," Lavin admitted. "Their actions could have created a stumbling block. So, for the general good of the workers, and the welfare of the Brotherhood, they had to be eliminated."

Excitement stirred in Holten's chest. He'd never played at being a Pinkerton man. In fact, he'd never had much use for the sleazy detectives. Now, he sensed some of what they must feel when closing in on a dangerous criminal.

"And . . . ?" he prompted.

A collective sigh came from the four men. Lavin carried on the narrative of murder.

"Liam and Devon took care of the first, O'Casey. Luke and his boys finished off the other two. Now, I think your little game of detective has gone on quite long enough, Holten."

The scout feigned innocence. "I don't know what you mean. I only wanted to learn how to make a union work."

Devon Flynn moved closer. The big-bellied, ham-fisted enforcer glowered at Eli, his jet black eyes afire with blood lust. His right hand rested on the black, hard rubber grips of a Colt revolver sticking out of the waistband of his trousers.

"Did you actually believe we'd fall for that preposterous story?" Arthur Lavin taunted. "I've been a labor organizer since the movement started. Many of the, ah, Brotherhoods had no use for my, er, particular talents, or those of my associates. Our methods were considered too crude for their, ah, sensibilities."

"I see. There are good unions and then there's your kind."

"My kind, as you so sneeringly put it, are the ones which make the most money for those who control them. Many of the others go broke. Quite a few go to

205

jail under the clubs of the police." Fascinated by his own eloquence and confident of his superiority, Lavin rambled on.

"We've developed a system that insures such misfortunes do not occur. Our talents are in demand by a number of labor fronts."

"Such as the International Collective of Railroad Workers?"

"Precisely. For instance, I'm sure you saw Percy Throckmorton's handiwork? His genius with explosives has discouraged a great number of strike breakers in the past. Pity he's a flit. Then there's the marvelous way we eliminated dissension in the ranks. Even the Army's convinced the Cheyenne did it."

"What's happened to the people who ran this construction project?" Holten demanded.

"Unfortunately, they managed to evade us. They're over with the soldiers now. Since you are obviously not going to survive this interview, there's no risk in reminding you that there are a great deal more of us than soldiers right now. When the time comes, we'll simply take them back."

"This has all been most enlightening," the scout replied sarcastically.

"Yes. And I'm afraid we've run out of things to say. Luke, you and Devon figure out some imaginative way for our scout here to meet his end. Away from the railroad, of course. Something . . . colorful, if you follow?"

Rough hands grabbed at Eli Holten. He lashed out with both fists and swung a kick at Liam Daley's crotch. A tall clerk's desk crashed over as the labor organizer jumped backward to prevent serious injury. Holten connected with the side of Devon Flynn's head and sent the burly organizer staggering. Then thick arms encircled him and Luke Partridge's huge hands locked over his solar plexus.

Squeezing with all his might, the powerful hardcase drove the air from Holten's lungs. Black spots danced before Eli's eyes and his body spasmed in tormented need of oxygen. His restricted movements became more feeble and his chin sank to his chest.

"Get his six-gun," Lavin commanded.

Metal scraped on leather as Flynn removed the Remington from Eli's holster. It was the last sound Eli heard.

He could wait no longer. Tall Bear had not sent the signal as agreed. Spotted Horse edged his mount forward until he could see over the brow of the rise to the iron road. Three men came toward him. Two held a fourth by the arms. Eyes straining, Spotted Horse recognized Eli Holten. He raised his lance, glanced left and right at his warriors and swiftly lowered the feathered shaft.

"Yiiiiii! Mi-shii-ahtah!"

Eli Holten awakened to the sound of a screeching war cry, in the suddenly slackened grip of Liam Daley and Devon Flynn. Still groggy, he remained limp until he could evaluate his chances.

"Holy Mary, they're comin' again," Daley blurted out.

"Must be a hunnered o' the heathen bastards," Flynn babbled. "Christ, they're gonna kill us all."

Hoofbeats rumbled over the prairie, growing louder. Suddenly the frightened labor toughs let Eli drop to the spongy sod. Their companion, Luke Partridge, who had never seen an Indian attack before, began to run, bleating in terror.

"We ain't got time to deal with this one. Let the redskins finish him off."

"Aye. Let's get th' hell outta here."

Daley and Flynn had barely turned and started to flee toward the railroad tracks when Holten sprang from the ground. Pain exploded through them as the scout hurtled through the air feet first and, with powerful thrusts of his thighs, drove a moccasin into the small of each man's back.

Driven forward, the two enforcers bowled over on the grassy soil. Flynn tried to scramble to his feet, only to be caught under his chin by another kick. Eli Holten heard the dry-stick crackle of breaking bones and Devon Flynn began to flop and writhe on the ground in uncontrollable death throes. Instantly, the scout diverted his attention to Liam Daley.

Daley had clawed the revolver from the waistband of his trousers. Holten darted forward and lashed out with his left hand, knocking the six-gun off target. Powder grains stung Eli's cheek when the heavy Colt fired involuntarily. The loud blast tortured his ears. Ignoring it, the scout groped in the small pouch at his waist and brought out a Shattuck four shot palm pistol.

The diminutive .32 spat twice. Two black holes, half an inch apart, appeared on Liam Daley's forehead. His eyes bulged and he stood as though transfixed, while blood began to well from the entry wounds. The .45 Colt dropped from Daley's grasp and he gave a mighty shudder, before he crumpled to the earth. Eli bent to pick up the Peace Maker and started in the direction of the express car, after the frightened Luke Partridge.

Arrows moaned overhead as Eli covered ground in a rapid trot. Raucous war whoops blended with the whinnies of horses and the crackle of gunfire. Dust and powder smoke thickened into an impenetrable fog. When he neared the work train, Eli could make out voices, crying in panic.

"Where's the Army?"

"Why don't the soldiers help us?"

"How come there's so many Injuns?"

"Over here, over here. I'm hit with an arrow!"

"Oh, Christ, they're everywhere!"

Holten kept his eyes on his quarry. The thick-shouldered red-head lumbered over the irregular terrain in an unvarying line toward the protection of the train. Nearly there, he staggered to one side, pulling frantically on an arrow that wobbled in the back of his left arm. The scout exerted greater speed in an attempt to close with the man who had bear-hugged him.

Percy Throckmorton's hand trembled while he fitted a fuse cap into a stick of dynamite. His fourth since the attack began, he would soon have enough to make a noticeable difference in the tide of battle. Such a frightful sound the heathens made. It simply unnerved him to hear those wailing cries. His whole morning had been absolutely *ruined* by the howling brutes.

Such a pity, too. He had almost figured out a way to work himself into the good graces of the soldiers by going over to their side. Then he could continue his pursuit of that gorgeous little tow-headed lad. Ah, Timmy, Timmy. What an angelic face the sweet boy had. They could have great fun together, Percy knew from similar past experiences. Ever so delightful. No time for that, though. He had only one more charge to prepare.

Ready at last, Percy lined the six sticks of dynamite up on a tie, protruding from the stack, and produced a match. He scratched the lucifer to life and selected a charge. Gingerly, flinching at the noise of gunfire, he touched the flame to the frayed end of fuse. Once it began to sputter nicely, Percy rose up and brought back his arm to throw.

White agony seared through his body when an arrow buried deep in the right side of his chest. Reflexively, his fingers opened and the sizzling stick of explosive dropped to the ground. The dynamite forgotten, Percy squinted his eyes in pain and sought to remove the terrible cause from his brutalized flesh. Too late, he recalled the burning powder train. His mouth opened in a soundless scream of terror.

An instant later the dynamite exploded. Sympathetic detonation set off the other five sticks.

In a flash, there no longer remained enough pieces of Percy Throckmorton to sew together for a funeral.

In a dizzying blur, a Cheyenne warrior darted through the space between Luke Partridge and the express car. His lance held on the off-side, it ripped through Luke's leather vest and woolen shirt, slicing a hot, thin gash across his chest. Reeling away from the almost casual attack, mouth contorted in misery, Luke turned to see the scout only three paces from him.

Desperate and disordered, Luke Partridge tried to bring up Eli Holten's own Remington six-gun. Before his thumb looped over the hammer spur, the .45 Peace Maker in Eli's hand belched flame and smoke.

Someone had hit him in the chest with a sledge hammer, Luke Partridge thought confusedly. Terrible pain came from the burning spot a fraction of an inch below the lance wound. Strange, he considered detachedly, how cold it had become. And . . . it couldn't be night already!

Yet the darkness grew and grew. Until it swallowed him.

Eli Holten bent and recovered his favored Remington, then tucked the Colt into his belt. He hurrried on toward the work train.

Captain David Roberts heard the muted thumps of gunfire while still a good half-mile away. The Cheyenne must be stirring up a regular hell-hole for those railroaders. He sincerely hoped Spotted Horse could contain them enough so as not to create a future problem about treaty violations. All in all, a crazy idea Eli had. Though it might just work. He raised his right arm, bent at the elbow, and pumped it up and down in a signal to come to the gallop.

Davey didn't want to be late for the fun.

Rincón stood atop a boxcar, methodically pumping round after round from a Winchester .44-40. He saw a shower of blood fly from the head of the last Indian he had aimed at and waved the rifle above his head in wild celebration.

"Matale! Matale indios!" he shouted.

From behind, Rincón heard the heavy thuds of military Springfield carbines. The few cavalry in camp had begun to fight back also. A heavy .45-70 slug ripped a spray of splinters from the edge of the wooden walkway he stood upon. Angered, Rincón shook a fist at the distant soldiers.

"Estupido soldados cabrónes!" he yelled, then repeated himself in English. "Stupid asshole soldiers! You're shooting at us, not the Indians."

"I know it," a grinning trooper replied in a shout a moment before he fired a fat 405 grain slug that exploded Rincón's head into a shower of bone fragments, blood and pulpy brain tissue.

Ammunition ran low among the workmen. The

211

Cheyenne continued to menace them from all sides. Pressing in closer, the painted warriors inspired greater panic. In a desperate, final show of defiance, the last few rounds crackled from a meager dozen weapons. Then it became pick handles and spike mauls against war clubs and lances. Whooping delightedly, the Cheyenne braves surged in to count coup. Eli Holten ignored the unequal battle as he reached the steps up to the end door of the express car.

He found the portal locked against him. Undaunted, he took a step back, cocked his foot and slammed it against the wood beside the brass latch.

The panel swung inward with a loud crash, followed at once by the blast of the scout's Remington. Through undulating layers of smoke, Holten made out the crouching figures of Arthur Lavin and Ned McKeon. Both turned to fire at Eli, who dove out of the path of their bullets.

For the moment, stalemate.

Captain Dave Roberts raised in his stirrups. "Prepare to draw sabres . . . Draw sabres! Trumpeter sound the *Charge*."

Crisp and ringing, like Gabriel's final trump, the gloriously haunting notes of the cavalry charge rolled across the prairie. As it continued to peal ecstatically, the thunder of hoofs grew to an awesome crescendo.

"The cavalry! It's the cavalry, come to rescue us!" one beleaguered ballastman cried in a flood of relief.

"Look. Soldiers," bellowed another worker. "Get 'em boys! Go after those redskins!"

Sunlight flickered off the naked blades of the troopers' sabres, the dreaded 'long knives' that had struck fear before into the hearts of many plains tribes. This time, though, the Cheyenne gathered into a compact formation and waited while the soldiers galloped closer. In their midst, Spotted Horse raised his feathered lance and waved it cheerfully at the approaching cavalry. Then, with a whoop of delight, he and his warriors raced away from the tracks, headed westward.

Oblivious to this strange turn, Arthur Lavin called out from inside the express car. "You hear that, Holten? The cavalry. Yer a renegade, fightin' with the Cheyenne. And we can prove it. You're all through. You'll get a firing squad for this. So's Philliphant finished. The Platte River and Pacific is ruined. And the ICRW will get rich on the pickings!"

"Wrong, Lavin. Davey Roberts and I planned the whole little show with Spotted Horse for your entertainment. Now that you've admitted who's behind the murders, you haven't a chance. Throw down your guns and come out with your hands up. You'll get a fair trial."

"That'll be before or after they hang us? Not likely, Holten."

"We'd better do it, boss. It's that or die here fightin'," McKeon whined.

"I don't intend to hang or to die in this grubby car. Cover me. We're going out the side door and get away from here. But first, I'm going to finish off Holten."

"That's crazy."

"Do it or I'll gun you down, McKeon."

Arthur Lavin slid back the thick side door and jumped to the loose ballast. Immediately he began to run toward the rear of the car. Reluctantly, Ned McKeon followed. From ahead of them they could hear Eli Holten's voice.

"Last chance, Lavin. Come out or I'll come in and get you."

Arthur Lavin dashed around the back end of the car with his Bacon .38 Navy revolver blazing. One slug

213

gouged splinters from the wooden back wall. Another cut a hot path through buckskin, uncomfortably close to Eli's left arm pit. A third spanged off a round metal stanchion for the vestibule roof.

Flattened, it richocheted to the left and struck the scout in the side of his head. Eli Holten went down like a slaughtered steer, a welter of blood flying from under his hat. The battered, low-crown Stetson sailed into the air as Eli limply struck the floorboards, to lie frightfully still.

Chapter 23

Timmy Pruett heard the golden notes of the charge and watched in open-mouthed amazement as the cavalry swept over the prairie and thundered down on the Cheyenne. He couldn't believe it when the leader of each force saluted the other and the troopers let the Indians ride away unharmed. Even though he had wondered why the Cheyenne hadn't attacked the soldiers, he couldn't quite put it all together.

"Trumpeter, sound *Recall*," the handsome, blond-haired cavalry officer commanded.

Timmy looked to Archie and Brian in confusion. "What's goin' on?"

"Don't know for sure, but I'd be willin' to say that somehow the so'jers and the Cheyenne joined forces again' those spalpeen bastards who seized the railroad," Brian O'Dwyer offered.

Movement at the side of the work train attracted Timmy's attention. He recognized Arthur Lavin when the labor organizer jumped from the side door and started at a lope toward the rear platform. By now, Timmy had no doubts that Lavin and his evil companions had been responsible for the murder of his friend, Sean O'Casey. Anger boiled up in the boy's frail body. He tightly grasped the little .32-20 Savage rifle he had used before and came swiftly to his feet.

215

"Timmy! What'er ye doin' lad?" Brian called after him. "Come back here, boy."

Timmy ignored the appeal, intent on only one thing. Despite the appearance of another of the killers, he intended to get his revenge. His thin legs churned as he ran directly toward a point where he figured he would intersect with Lavin. Part way there he saw the tall, rugged frame of Eli Holten on the rear platform. Timmy's steps faltered, uncertain now of his chosen course. It gave Lavin time to reach the rear of the car.

Gunfire erupted in a frenzy only a second later. Timmy saw Eli fall and heard Lavin's triumphant shout.

"You're dead, you bastard!"

Timmy had only thirty feet to cover. He sprinted with the speed of an antelope. Ballast showered in front of the lad as he set his feet and stopped. He jerked up the little game rifle at point blank range and squeezed the trigger.

"Die you son of a bitch!" he shrilled in his high, thin voice.

Startled, Lavin had half turned and thrown up his right arm in the moment when the .32-20 Savage detonated. The 100 grain slug entered his body in the right arm pit. Deflected by a rib, it pulped a large portion of the upper lobe of his right lung, turned downward and pierced his diaphragm near the outer edge. It stopped, flattened and missing fragments of lead, against the inner flare of Lavin's hip bone.

Arthur Lavin sat abruptly. Fresh white chunks of ballast clattered away from him, gruesomely decorated with spatters of red. Eyes blurring, Arthur Lavin looked at his executioner. A kid. A skinny, snot-nosed brat. His mouth worked like a beached fish, which sent a crimson tide of blood pouring from his lips. His astonishment became almost too much to overcome.

"All . . . all this . . . way," Arthur Lavin rasped. "Only . . . only to . . . to be k-killed by . . . a kid."

Tears had begun to stream down Timmy's face. Ignoring McKeon, he ran past the man he had shot, to climb urgently onto the platform. Eli Holten lay in a sprawl. Blood poured from the side of his head. A soulful groan escaped from Timmy's twisted mouth. He came to his feet again and climbed off the train. He walked up close to Arthur Lavin.

"That was for Sean," Timmy's quavering voice informed the downed man as the boy raised his rifle once more. "This is for Eli Holten."

Again the Savage barked. The bullet popped through Arthur Lavin's right eyesocket and exploded his existence in a shower of bright sparks. Ned McKeon had dropped his rifle and fallen to his knees. He raised his hands in mute surrender, a pitiful whine escaping his lips, eyes white with terror.

A shot sounded to Timmy's left and the slug slammed into McKeon's head, through his spittle-dripping mouth. The force of the impact knocked both of his eyes from their sockets. The corpse flung backward and twitched in the gravel. Timmy's shoulder slumped and he began to sob.

Then, from behind him, he heard a shuddering moan. The boy stiffened, half-turned. Hope burst within his skinny chest. Another dazed groan. With the Savage .32-20 held carelessly in one hand, Timmy ran to the platform and scrambled up.

"He's alive!" he shouted jubilantly a second later. "Eli Holten's alive!"

"Spotted Horse, together we have won a great victory," Sterling Philliphant told the Cheyenne war leader some two hours later. He and Captain Roberts had met

217

the young chief in a temporary camp five miles from the railhead.

"To commemorate it, I have decided to add one more term to my offer to you."

"You are a brave man to ride beside, Phil-pant. And a generous one. I would ask what's this new term you speak of?"

"If we are agreed. If my railroad can pass through Cheyenne country in peace, I promise that forever, so long as the trains shall run, that no piece of land along the right-of-way shall ever be sold to a white man, uh, a *nia'tha*. That property, from now on, can be owned only by Cheyenne."

"What is is to 'own'?"

Sterling Philliphant and Dave Roberts chuckled. "To have a piece of paper, Spotted Horse," the president of the railroad explained, "that proves the ground is yours and no one else can ever take it away. It is the way of the white man to protect that which he claims as his."

The Cheyenne chief thought a moment. "It is a good way. And you shall have your railroad, Phil-pant. I only wish our friend Tall Bear could be here."

"He's alive at least, thank God," Dave Roberts put in. "And mending well, the doctor says. He should, he has a good nurse."

"Nurse?"

"A woman who helps our medicine men cure the sick. In this case, a pretty one."

Spotted Horse smiled at Captain Roberts, then at Sterling Philliphant. "That's a good thing. Now, let us feast our victory."

The three men clasped forearms in Cheyenne fashion and started off toward the entrancing odor of roasting buffalo.

Eli Holten opened his eyes and made a soft, murmuring sound deep in his throat. He hurt like hell. Yet the therapy being carried out on him gave the scout strong indications that he would mend quickly and without much pain. His eyes roved around the fancy decorations of the sleeping compartment of the Philliphant private car. At last they fixed on his earnest healer.

Gwen Philliphant sat on the edge of Eli's bunk bed. Her left hand and arm extended under the blanket, fingers wrapped tightly around his swollen organ. She stroked it up and down in a rapid, even pace. At last she wet moist lips and spoke lightly.

"Looks like there's life in you after all, Eli."

"That feels wonderful."

"It should," she said snappishly. "I've been at it for nearly half an hour. In fact, I think I'm going to quit."

"Don't! Oh, don't do that."

"That's exactly what I shall do."

She released his rigid phallus and rose to her feet. Swiftly Gwen raised her dress and divested herself of her underclothes. Then she straddled the surprised scout and whisked away the blanket.

Reddened and ready, his long, silken shaft prodded the air. Slowly, Gwen lowered herself until she felt the ecstasy of contact with the broad tip of his mighty engine. Bit by bit she impaled herself on its goodness, excited anew by the tangible evidence of his own delicious response. Her hips swayed and she cooed with happiness as she accepted the last of his bold flesh.

"Ah, Eli, Eli, my love. I nearly died when they told me you had been shot in the head."

"Nothing to worry about. Wrong head, my dear," he teased.

"Eli!" she wailed. "That's awful. I may never make love with you again."

219

"Before or after this time?"

"After! Definitely after," she squeaked in heightening bliss as his magnificent manhood began to thrust deeply in and out of her burning passage. "Oh, Eli! Ooooh! Eliiii!"

"I think I'm going to enjoy this cure," the scout murmured playfully before he abandoned himself to the unbounded pleasure of her young and wanton body.

BOLT

An Adult Western Series by Cort Martin

#10: BAWDY HOUSE SHOWDOWN	(1176, $2.25)
#11: THE LAST BORDELLO	(1224, $2.25)
#12: THE HANGTOWN HARLOTS	(1274, $2.25)
#13: MONTANA MISTRESS	(1316, $2.25)
#14: VIRGINIA CITY VIRGIN	(1360, $2.25)
#15: BORDELLO BACKSHOOTER	(1411, $2.25)
#16: HARDCASE HUSSY	(1513, $2.25)
#17: LONE-STAR STUD	(1632, $2.25)
#18: QUEEN OF HEARTS	(1726, $2.25)
#19: PALOMINO STUD	(1815, $2.25)
#20: SIX-GUNS AND SILK	(1866, $2.25)

Available wherever paperbacks are sold, or order direct from the Publisher. Send cover price plus 50¢ per copy for mailing and handling to Zebra Books, Dept. 1898, 475 Park Avenue South, New York, N.Y. 10016. Residents of New York, New Jersey and Pennsylvania must include sales tax. DO NOT SEND CASH.

GREAT WESTERNS
by Dan Parkinson

THE SLANTED COLT   (1413, $2.25)
A tall, mysterious stranger named Kichener gave young
Benjamin Franklin Blake a gift. It was a gun, a colt pistol,
that had belonged to Ben's father. And when a cold-
blooded killer vowed to put Ben six feet under, it was a sure
thing that Ben would have to learn to use that gun—or die!

GUNPOWDER GLORY   (1448, $2.50)
Jeremy Burke, breaking a deathbed promise to his pa,
killed the lowdown Sutton boy who was the cause of his
pa's death. But when the bullets started flying, he found
there was more at stake than his own life as innocent
people were caught in the crossfire of *Gunpowder Glory.*

BLOOD ARROW   (1549, $2.50)
Randall Kerry returned to his camp to find his companion
slaughtered and scalped. With a war cry as wild as the savages', the young scout raced forward with his pistol held
high to meet them in battle.

BROTHER WOLF   (1728, $2.95)
Only two men could help Lattimer run down the sheriff's
killers—a stranger named Stillwell and an Apache who was
as deadly with a Colt as he was with a knife. One of them
would see justice done—from the muzzle of a six-gun.

CALAMITY TRAIL   (1663, $2.95)
Charles Henry Clayton fled to the west to make his fortune, get married and settle down to a peaceful life. But
the situation demanded that he strap on a six-gun and ride
toward a showdown of gunpowder and blood that would
send him galloping off to either death or glory on the . . .
Calamity Trail.

*Available wherever paperbacks are sold, or order direct from the
Publisher. Send cover price plus 50¢ per copy for mailing and
handling to Zebra Books, Dept. 1898, 475 Park Avenue South,
New York, N.Y. 10016. Residents of New York, New Jersey and
Pennsylvania must include sales tax. DO NOT SEND CASH.*

TALES OF THE OLD WEST

SPIRIT WARRIOR (1795, $2.50)
by G. Clifton Wisler
The only settler to survive the savage indian attack was a little boy. Although raised as a red man, every man was his enemy when the two worlds clashed—but he vowed no man would be his equal.

IRON HEART (1736, $2.25)
by Walt Denver
Orphaned by an indian raid, Ben vowed he'd never rest until he'd brought death to the Arapahoes. And it wasn't long before they came to fear the rider of vengeance they called . . . Iron Heart.

WEST OF THE CIMARRON (1681, $2.50)
by G. Clifton Wisler
Eric didn't have a chance revenging his father's death against the Dunstan gang until a stranger with a fast draw and a dark past arrived from West of the Cimarron.

HIGH LINE RIDER (1615, $2.50)
by William A. Lucky
In Guffey Creek, you either lived by the rules made by Judge Breen and his hired guns—or you didn't live at all. So when Holly took sides against the Judge, it looked like there would be just one more body for the buzzards. But this time they were wrong.

GUNSIGHT LODE (1497, $2.25)
by Virgil Hart
When Ned Coffee cornered Glass and Corey in a mine shaft, the last thing Glass expected was for the kid to make a play for the gold. And in a blazing three-way shootout, both Corey and Coffee would discover how lightening quick Glass was with a gun.